Rodeo Daughter

LEIGH DUNCAN

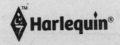

TORONTO NEW YORK LONDON
AMSTERDAM PARIS SYDNEY HAMBURG
STOCKHOLM ATHENS TOKYO MILAN MADRID
PRAGUE WARSAW BUDAPEST AUCKLAND

Recycling programs
for this product may
not exist in your area.

ISBN-13: 978-0-373-75410-6

RODEO DAUGHTER

Copyright © 2012 by Linda Duke Duncan

ABOUT THE AUTHOR

Award-winning author Leigh Duncan writes the kind of books she loves to read—ones where home, family and community are key to the happy endings we all deserve. Married to the love of her life and mother of two wonderful young adults, Leigh lives on central Florida's east coast.

When she isn't busy working on her next story for Harlequin American Romance, Leigh loves nothing better than to curl up in her favorite chair with a cup of hot coffee and a great book. She invites readers to follow her on Twitter or Facebook. Contact her at P.O. Box 410787, Melbourne, FL 32941 or visit her online at www.leighduncan.com.

Books by Leigh Duncan
HARLEQUIN AMERICAN ROMANCE

For Sandy
And all who dream of growing up to be real cowgirls.

Chapter One

"You've got to be kidding." Amanda leaned against the hood of her car. Staring into her father's perpetual blue-eyed squint, she fought for composure.

"Sorry, Mandy." Tom Markette managed to say the words without sounding or looking at all apologetic. "I need the biggest paycheck I can get, and Okeechobee offered it. Gas and feed ain't free, you know."

Amanda swallowed a bitter retort. There was more than money behind her father's decision to leave her twisting in the wind, and they both knew it. But this wasn't the time to dredge up old hurts. She shoved a hank of loose hair behind her ear and chose a different battle. She had more immediate issues to deal with, starting with the Saddle Up Stampede in…

"Dad, the stampede is in five days. *Five days.* You can't back out now."

Expecting to find her father in the practice ring of the Boots and Spurs Dude Ranch, where the bar association held its annual fundraiser, she'd closed her law office in nearby Melbourne and driven out to watch him ride. The instant she'd spotted his long form propped against his motor home, a familiar sinking feeling had formed in the pit of her stomach. Acid had burned the back of her throat when she'd spied a horse standing in the hitched-up trailer.

"Okeechobee lost their opening act and I took the job, baby girl. You know how it is. I have to take advantage of every opportunity." Tom speared her with a calculating glance. "If you'd give up this foolish notion and join the team again, I wouldn't have these problems."

There it was. Eight years, and her dad still hadn't forgiven her for walking away from the Markette Ropin' Team. Well, he wasn't the only one who bore a grudge. She held up a hand.

"You're the one backing out of our deal. Don't even try to lay this on me."

She eyed the man who should be standing with his hat in his hand, gratitude showing in his lined face for the easy paycheck he would earn putting on a roping-and-riding exhibition at the charity fundraiser. Hoping to impress him with the clout she wielded as the newest member of the bar association, she'd given him the job. But her father didn't appear grateful, much less impressed. If anything, he looked as if he couldn't wait to hit the road. And if he cared one whit about the predicament his leaving would put her in, it didn't show in the jaunty angle of the Stetson he'd perched on his head.

"By the time the show starts, three thousand people will be sitting right up there. Waiting for you, Dad." Amanda gestured toward the grandstand, which would be filled to capacity in less than a week. "How can you let them down?"

She didn't bother to ask how he could let *her* down. The fact was, neither of her folks had ever won a Parent of the Year award or shown any interest in her outside the rodeo ring. Their neglect had shaped her decision to specialize in family law, where her focus was always on the best interests of the child.

"Guess they'll have to settle for someone else." Tom Markette pushed himself away from his truck and reached out as if to hug her goodbye.

Amanda crossed her arms. "What, you think rodeo stars are hiding behind every palmetto bush? Or waiting in the barn till I call their number? No such luck."

And where did that leave her?

She was in charge of entertainment for this year's stampede. Come Saturday night, an empty arena was not an option. Not with her practice in its infancy and her reputation at stake. Not with every paralegal, attorney and judge in the county expecting the thrill and excitement of the best that rodeo had to offer. Not with at-risk kids up and down the east coast of Florida dependent on the money the event would raise.

"Ahh, Mandy. You always did worry too much. Royce and the rest of the crew'll still be here, won't they?"

They'd do some pole-bending rides, give a calf-roping demonstration. She'd lined up a live band and a country dance. All of which were small potatoes compared to the best roping-and-riding exhibition in the business. He was the headliner and the reason they'd sold so many advance tickets.

"Dad," she said pointedly, "you signed a contract. You're legally obligated to be here."

"Yeah, well, so sue me, baby girl. I won't be." He laughed easily, his smile so charming Amanda caught herself wanting to please him, to persuade him to stay, to be proud of her.

Old news.

She stifled a groan. He had her over a barrel and he

knew it. She'd no more sue her own father for breach of contract than she'd pick up the reins of the life she'd left behind. The only surprise was that, this time, she'd actually expected him to keep his word. She'd never forgive him for breaking it…again.

Her father tipped his hat back and gazed at her thoughtfully.

"All right, here's the deal. I already unloaded Brindle. Left him in a stall right over there." He thrust a thumb over his shoulder toward the Boots and Spurs stables. "I'll leave him with you through the weekend. I'll even swing by to pick him up on Sunday." Her dad made it sound as if he was doing her a huge favor. "You can take my place, ride him in the show."

Amanda stared from behind dark sunglasses. Was he crazy? Sure, she'd helped him design the roping and riding act he'd performed ever since injuries forced him out of the chase for the next big purse, the next gold buckle. But she'd put herself through college and law school since then.

"Dad, I haven't been riding. Not in months. I've been too busy getting the practice off the ground. I have clients who are counting on me."

Including one who had hired her that very morning. The custody battle between an admittedly prodigal mom and the father who'd had sole custody of their four-year-old deserved Amanda's full attention. She needed to dig into the heart of the case, figure out why no other family law attorney in town would touch it. She sensed this one could be a game changer, that success would give her prominence on the highly competitive playing field.

Her father clapped his hands, eager to hit the road.

Heading for the truck's cab, he spoke as if he hadn't listened to a word she'd said.

Which, Amanda realized, he hadn't.

"You'll be fine. I haven't changed the routine since the last time you saw it." He winked at her and slid onto the driver's seat. "Brindle knows it so well, all you'll have to do is hold on and let him do his thing. And who knows? Maybe you'll enjoy it so much, you'll chuck this life and come with me next time."

The big diesel engine sprang to life. The camper and trailer it towed lurched forward. Amanda's protests sputtered to a halt as the dust clouds settled in its wake.

With less than a week before the mini rodeo that was really more an exhibition than a competition, it was too late to find a replacement. She was stuck with the job. It wasn't as if she'd never been on a horse before. She had. She even had her own gold buckle to show for the years of sacrifice and training, years she'd spent trying to earn her father's love.

"Don't go there," she whispered.

There were other places she needed to be, though, things she needed to do. She made a list and started checking off the items one by one on her way to the stables. Knowing the first order of business was to clear her calendar, she tugged her cell phone from her back pocket and left a message for her secretary.

The familiar scents of hay and horseflesh filled her nose as Amanda stepped from bright sunshine and stifling heat into the relative cool of the stables. From the third stall down on the left, a horse nickered. A large pale head leaned out over the door. Amanda ran a hand over the horse's neck and felt the palomino quiver.

"Hey, big guy," she whispered to her dad's second-best mount. "It's been a while. You remember me?"

The horse snorted and nudged her shoulder, looking for a treat.

"That's a good boy," Amanda said. She might have put the rodeo scene behind her, but some things never changed. She pulled the expected handful of carrots from her pocket.

Blowing soft wet kisses, Brindle lipped them from her open palm.

"You ready for a little run?" she asked the horse.

Spangles glinted from the saddle her dad had tossed over one wall of the chest-high pen. A pile of blankets, bridles and other tack sat beneath it. Amanda straightened the fringe on a costume of soft caramel buckskin she hadn't seen in years. She shook her head. Her father had thought of everything, eliminated every reason why she couldn't take his place.

Well, except that maybe she was so out of practice she'd have trouble sitting in the saddle, much less standing on top of it while Brindle thundered across the arena. She gave a final thought to the case that had landed in her lap earlier that morning, and sighed. There was a ton of work to do in the two weeks before she and her client made their first courtroom appearance.

But all that would have to wait until Sunday morning, when the performance she'd never wanted to give was behind her.

MITCHELL GOODWIN LIFTED the miniscule teacup from the wooden table in the playroom. Shifting uncomfortably on the narrow painted bench, he raised the tiny piece of china, tipped an imaginary toast to his hostess and pretended to drink.

"Yum." His cup rattled into its saucer. "Hailey, that hit the spot. Thank you so much."

Across the table, a frown clouded a pair of brilliant blue eyes. Mitch noted the purse of rosebud lips, and leaned forward.

"What's wrong, sweetheart?"

"You forgot to crook-ed your pinkie, Daddy. Mrs. Birch says it's a rule." Four-year-old Hailey Goodwin demonstrated. "Now your turn, Daddy."

Beneath the tiny picnic table, the pointed toe of Mitch's left boot pinched. He flexed his ankle to stave off a muscle cramp brought on by the longer-than-usual tea party. Cup in hand, finger properly bent this time, he took another sip.

"Wait! Your cup is empty. Put it down here." Hailey pointed to a doll-size serving tray. "I'll pour some more."

Hoping to goodness that the exorbitant tuition he paid to Mrs. Birch's Angel Care covered a lot more than lessons in etiquette, Mitch held out his cup as his daughter poured make-believe tea from a tiny china pot.

"Did your class sing the A-B-C song, honey? Did you practice your letters?"

"Would you like a cookie, Daddy?" Hailey held out a small plate filled with plastic wafers. "They're coconut. Mrs. Birch says they're the bestest kind."

Uh-oh.

Mitch's smile froze. When he'd stocked up on treats for the evening, coconut hadn't been on his shopping list.

"The best, huh? Last week, you asked for chocolate chip."

"Did you buy some?" Her eyes going wide, Hailey stared over his shoulder at the door to the kitchen.

"There's a brand-new box on the counter. I bought them especially for you and Betty Jean."

Hailey's fists landed on her sturdy little hips. "Why does she have to be here, Daddy? I want you to tuck me in, same as always."

"Hailey, remember your promise." An hour of dolls and stories were his part of the bargain. In exchange, Hailey had promised to behave for the babysitter. Lifting his cup again, Mitch blew out air that he hoped his daughter took for a cooling breath and not an exasperated sigh. Life wasn't fair, and little girls—even ones without mothers—couldn't have their way *all* the time. "We talked about this," he reminded his daughter when her glower continued. "Betty Jean will help you say your prayers, but I'll kiss you good-night before I leave, and again after I come home. You'll get lots of kisses."

"And cookies?" Hailey asked, the picture of innocence.

Mitch bit back a laugh and shook his head. There were a few consolations to having a wife who'd abandoned her newborn to run off with another man. Karen hadn't stuck around long enough to teach their daughter the fine art of manipulation.

"You know the rules." Too much sugar and Hailey wouldn't sleep well. "Just one."

Dark curls spilled onto her face, nearly hiding the gleam in her eyes. "If I'm extra good, can I have more?"

His daughter drove a hard bargain. Someday she'd make a good lawyer, just like her father, and his father before him. His resolve weakening, Mitch answered, "Two. But only if you play nice with Betty Jean."

"I will, Daddy," Hailey said solemnly.

The storm that had gathered in his child's face dissipated. This time, Mitch didn't bother to try to hide his relief. His attendance at the bar association's charity event was not optional. The district attorney might not stand at the gate with a clipboard or check names off a list, but the man would soon name his successor. As his protégé, Mitch expected to get the nod. Now was not the time to slip up by skipping an important appearance.

Besides, he practically had an obligation to speak with the star of tonight's show, didn't he? Sure, he'd been only sixteen that summer he'd worked as a counselor at Camp Bridle Catch. But he hadn't forgotten the long days in the saddle, any more than he'd forgotten the green-eyed girl who'd stolen his heart the night they'd slipped away to a carnival in town. He tapped a finger against his lips, recalling the wonder of that first kiss, and the others they'd shared during long nights around the campfire. Though their love hadn't survived past the summer, he'd followed her meteoric rise on the rodeo circuit. When she'd suddenly retired eight years ago, he'd wondered why. Tonight, he'd finally have a chance to ask Tom Markette about his daughter.

Strictly as one old friend asking about another, of course.

Mitch shot the cuff of a suitably Western-style shirt and checked his watch just as chimes signaled the arrival of the babysitter. Hailey's little-girl laughter rang through the room. Their tea party abruptly forgotten, she charged toward the front door.

In the entryway, where stick-figure artwork crowded the walls, Mitch motioned Betty Jean into the air-conditioning that made life on Florida's east coast bearable. The college student was familiar with their routines, so once Hailey calmed down enough for him to get a word in edgewise, he made quick work of the necessary instructions.

"There's leftover spaghetti, mac 'n cheese, chicken tenders or fish sticks for supper." He rattled off the list of Hailey's current favorites. "Cookies for dessert. She can have a couple." He waited until Hailey's back was turned to signal that three would be okay.

"I'll be home before midnight," he whispered, wary of last-minute objections.

He needn't have worried.

Betty Jean pulled bottles of glittery nail polish from her backpack, earning herself a big tip and his daughter's instant devotion. Soon, the girls were chatting like magpies as they cleared away the tea things to make room for a manicure station. And when Mitch bent to deliver the promised good-night kiss, Hailey barely offered her cheek with a, "Bye, Daddy, see ya later," before asking the babysitter which polish matched her outfit.

Seeing his child engrossed in the girlie stuff he didn't quite understand, Mitch rubbed at an empty spot in his chest. For the moment, he shoved the feeling aside. But weaving his way through rows of cars parked on a grassy field twenty minutes later, he couldn't avoid second-guessing his plans for the night. Now that his ex-wife had breezed back into town demanding not just a place in their child's life, but full custody, should he have stayed home, tried harder to be both mother and father to his little girl?

The heel of one cowboy boot caught a divot in the grass, and his other foot came down hard. The move jarred Mitch, and he smiled, thinking it might have knocked some sense back into him. He was a prominent attorney. He'd worked hard to make a good home for Hailey. While he couldn't guarantee the judge's ruling, he could definitely prove he was a better parent than the woman who hadn't called or visited her child in four years.

His thoughts settled, he stopped by the Boots and Spurs barn, where a band was setting up for the dance following the rodeo. Making his way past scattered hay bales and picnic benches, he dutifully checked out the silent auction part of the fundraising event. This year's prizes ranged from a dance with one of the rodeo stars to riding lessons. Since Hailey would enjoy the latter, he scribbled down a bid before dropping a generous check in the donation box.

Then it was on to the arena, where he plunged into a milling throng. He bought a bag of freshly roasted peanuts from a vendor, and worked his way toward the stands, chatting with people he knew, greeting some he didn't. He traded nods with Randall Hill, the county's district attorney, before taking a seat in the reserved section. Mitch had barely settled into it when a cowboy on a gray horse raced onto the dirt track, quickly wove between several flagpoles, and sped back the way he'd come.

Top-notch entertainment?

Maybe not, Mitch decided as he cracked a few peanut shells. By the end of his summer at rodeo camp, he'd ridden nearly as well. He smiled, remembering how Mandy had taken pity on his inexperience and given him a few pointers on calf roping. He'd spent the next six weeks head-over-heels for her. His thoughts drifted to the stolen hours they'd spent in each other's arms. The innocence of those days helped keep his fears about the looming custody case at bay. Or so he told himself, until the arena emptied and he realized he'd been so lost in thought he'd missed the warm-up acts.

"We're sorry to hafta tell ya'll that Tom Markette can't be with us tonight," a voice drawled over the loud-speakers. "But we got a real treat for ya. Takin' his place is one time-member of the Markette Ropin' Team and a champ-een barrel racer in her own right…Ma-a-and-y Mar-ket-t-te."

Mitch searched the ring below. Had he heard correctly? Or had the flood of memories about his first love tricked his ears into deceiving him?

As he watched, an elaborately costumed blonde calmly made her way to the center of the arena astride a large and equally bedecked golden horse. Mitch's gaze narrowed in on the rider as the pair turned, giving him his first good look at the woman Mandy had become. Gone was the coltish figure of that long-ago summer, replaced by womanly curves. Horse and rider stood still for several long seconds, until a hush fell over the crowd.

Then, without warning, Mandy let loose a rebel yell. Dirt sprayed from the horse's hooves. The big palomino raced through a dizzying series of figure eights. Coming out of a final turn, the rider called, "Hee-yah!"

Instantly, the horse beneath her surged into a full gallop.

Mitch stared, unwilling to move, hardly daring to breathe. His heart pounded while Mandy danced in the saddle, sometimes standing, sometimes leaning so far over her long braids brushed the ground. When she wheeled for the final run, everyone in the crowd surged to their feet. Mitch scrambled to his, glad for the extra few inches that let him see over those in front.

Below, a broad smile on her face, her arms spread wide, Mandy stood atop the prancing palomino. While the crowd roared in approval, horse and rider raced for the gate.

All too soon the last dirt clod settled to the ground. By the time a rodeo clown stepped into the arena, doffed a ten-gallon Stetson and latched the gate, Mitch's feet were in motion. With every step he took closer to the barn, his plans firmed. He would attend the dance and talk shop with the law clerks who lingered around the punch bowl. But first, he'd enter a bid in the silent auction. One high enough to win a dance with the star of tonight's rodeo.

HEART PUMPING, limbs trembling from the exertion, Amanda slid from Brindle's saddle, patted the horse soundly and slipped him a couple of well-deserved sugar cubes. The big palomino snorted in pleasure, and she gave him a hug. Together, they had nailed it. Delivered the performance of a lifetime. So what if the ride hadn't been quite flawless? The applause from the grandstand proved that no one at the Saddle Up Stampede cared if she'd lost her hat halfway through the second cloverleaf. Or nearly lost her footing as she rode out of the arena.

"Be sure you walk him until he cools off." She handed Brindle's reins to a waiting stable hand. "Then give him an extra measure of oats and a long rubdown."

Lucky horse. His work was done. Hers, not so much.

The sawing screech of an out-of-tune fiddle drifted across the parking lot, a reminder of the country dance that would end the evening's festivities. Her pulse still racing on the high of a near-perfect ride, Amanda spun on a boot heel. The barn, where cowboy hats bobbed on a sea of plaid shirts above straight-legged Levi's, beckoned.

At a gingham-covered table, she asked about the winning bid for the first dance.

"Great show, Amanda." The auctioneer beamed. "You musta' made an impression on Mitchell Goodwin." He pointed to the dark-haired man who strode toward them from the cashier's booth.

Mitch? Now, that was a name she hadn't expected. Memories rose like smoke from the campfire she and Mitch had once cuddled beside. They'd gazed at the stars and talked for hours, and ended up falling in love.

Frowning at her exaggerated version of puppy love, Amanda swallowed a wave of nostalgia. At sixteen, Mitch had been all knobby knees and elbows. Tonight, there was nothing awkward about the man whose long strides brought him ever closer. Laugh lines around his mouth enhanced his broad smile. Her own lips curved upward as she noted his familiar straight nose and high cheekbones, and her breath hitched when their eyes met. His were so deep that, for a moment, she let herself get lost in their azure depths, the way she had one summer night as they stood in line for the Ferris wheel. How had she ever forgotten eyes such a vibrant blue? Or the way his quick smile had once thrilled her heart? She'd kept a diary that summer, each page crammed with inky script, their initials entwined along the edges.

She gave him her best smile. "It's good to see you, Mitch."

"Mandy." His focus never wavered as he extended a hand. "It's been too long."

She'd left the nickname behind the day she'd walked away from professional rodeo, but mentioning that now seemed petty. Slipping her fingers into his warm grasp, she was surprised by the pinprick of heartbreak that lingered after all these years. The urge to move closer faded.

Mitch had always had an uncanny way of reading her thoughts. Now, he stepped back, relinquishing his hold. "Well, you've certainly come a long way since rodeo camp."

His slow, appraising glance skimmed over her like a caress.

"I always knew you would. You put on a great show tonight." His smile widened into a teasing grin. "I guess you hear that all the time."

"Not so often anymore, but you always did *say* the nicest things."

Her sarcasm surprised Amanda almost as much as the embarrassed look that passed quickly over Mitch's face. Her throat tightened, and she cleared it. His smile had dredged up memories of the kisses they'd shared... and the hurt that had followed. She raced to think of a topic that might steer the conversation away from painful adolescent memories.

"I guess you stuck with the plan and went into law." She gestured toward the crowd of bar association members who stood around in tight knots, waiting for the dance to start. "What's your specialty?"

"I'm with the district attorney's office."

His answer explained the air of authority he carried on his wide shoulders. She nodded, understanding why they hadn't run into each other. So far, her work hadn't required a visit to the courthouse's criminal division.

Before she had a chance to mention her own practice, the band finished their warm-ups and ran through the opening bars of "Arkansas Traveler." On the plywood stage, Mark Jansen, president of the bar association, stepped to the microphone. Throughout the barn, chatter quieted, except when someone in the back yelled "Let's hear some music!" The call echoed off the rafters.

Jansen grinned, waiting until a spate of laughter died down before promising to keep his remarks brief. After assuring everyone that their contributions would appear in the next edition of the *Bar News,* he revealed the amount they'd raised for charities catering to at-risk children. The evening's total was impressive enough that several wolf whistles punctuated a round of applause.

"That's four thousand more than we raised last year. In this economy, you've truly outdone yourselves." He signaled the band. "And now, our own Mitchell Goodwin will lead tonight's star performer, Mandy Markette, in the first dance. Ya'll join in, y'hear."

Her hand tucked in Mitch's grasp, Amanda followed the good-looking attorney out onto the straw-covered dance floor. She'd barely turned to face him before the fiddle player led them into a slow rendition of "Rodeo Moon."

"Shall we?" Mitch bowed ever so slightly.

With a reminder that the night was all about charity, Amanda plastered on a broad smile and ignored her misgivings about stepping into Mitch's arms again. She told herself they certainly wouldn't fit together as well as they had one long-ago summer. She was a different person from the girl he'd known back then. Plus, in the intervening years Mitch had grown several inches taller. At six-feet-something, he now towered over her compact frame.

But two measures into the waltz, Mitch slipped his arm around her waist. The gentle press of his hand sent familiar tingles up and down her spine.

Struggling to hide a rush of heat, Amanda pressed her cheek to his chest. His woodsy aftershave mingled with a faint powdery smell she couldn't quite identify. Whatever it was, it triggered a wave of longing for the home her childhood on the road had never included. She inhaled deeper while the singer belted out a song that made the rodeo circuit sound far more romantic than the life she'd known.

All too soon, the notes of the first number faded. Mitch's smoldering eyes met hers, and Amanda knew with one glance that he wanted to continue their time together. When he motioned toward one of the barn's big doors, she barely hesitated. She ducked outside, feeling giddy, while he grabbed two cups of punch from a table decked out like a chuck wagon. They moved into the shadows beyond the light that spilled from the door, not stopping until they'd left the acrid odor of several cigarette smokers behind. In a quiet spot, they leaned against a hitching rail.

"I can't believe you're really here. I'd planned to ask your dad about you after the show, but *seeing* you is so much better." Concern dimmed the light in Mitch's eyes. "He ever straighten up? Become the father you needed him to be?"

Amanda stifled an angry reply. No matter how much she'd changed, some things remained the same—and her dad was one of them. After her mom died, he'd dumped Amanda in rodeo camp and toured the country, preferring to rope and ride alone than help her deal with her grief. Meeting Mitch had been the only bright spot that terrible summer, and her dad had been the topic of more than one conversation between them.

She rolled her eyes. "He's still up to the same old tricks. He backed out of the Saddle Up Stampede at the last minute, conned me into riding in his place. How about yourself? Did you go back to Camp Bridle Catch the next year?"

"Nah, that was the last in a long line of summer

camps. It was all college prep and internships after that."

Their lives couldn't have been more different. For her, the next few years had been about winning a gold buckle in Las Vegas.

Amanda drained the cup Mitch handed her and set it aside. Talking to him brought back all her old hurts. It was as if she'd been asleep for years and had now been shaken awake, her adrenaline pumping for a fight. The urge to give Mitch a piece of her mind warred with the desire to grab him and hug him. She wasn't sure where to start. In the end, she decided to rip the bandage off by tackling their breakup.

"I waited for you in the stables like we'd planned that last day of camp. You never showed."

Mitch propped his arms on the top rail beside hers. "I couldn't. My parents were furious—and probably embarrassed—that Ben and I had gotten into a fight. They refused to listen when I tried to explain. Instead, they marched us to the car. We were halfway to the Grand Canyon before I got a chance to state my case."

"You never called. Never wrote."

"I wanted to. I scoured the internet for the Markette Ropin' Team. What little information I could find was always about where you'd been, not where you were headed. I'm sorry we never got to say goodbye."

Amanda nodded, finally understanding why Mitch had left her alone and confused and, after an hour, madder than a wet cat.

"What was that all about, anyway? I never understood why you and your brother got into it like that."

"Guy stuff." Mitch shrugged. "Teen guy stuff," he corrected. "Ben made some crack about my hot girlfriend. Before I knew it, he was on the ground and I was standing there, daring him to get up."

Amanda laughed when Mitch gently elbowed her ribs.

"Oh. So, your brother thought I was hot, did he?"

His quiet "You still are" made her heart beat double time. Not quite ready to pick up where they'd left off as teenagers, she reminded herself that she didn't know the man he'd become. She changed the subject.

"How'd you wind up in Melbourne? I thought you'd settle in Savannah near your folks." As a teen, Mitch had talked about joining the family law practice.

"I did for a while. Almost made partner in Goodwin & Sons before..." Mitch's shoulders straightened. "Things changed. Dad's firm specializes in defense work. I got one of his clients off on a technicality. Turned out the guy was guilty. The next time he robbed a liquor store, somebody got hurt. I took a job with the state attorney's office and moved here soon after."

"Oh." Amanda sighed. "That must have been rough." His plans had changed as much as hers had. Back when they'd known each other, she'd wanted nothing more than to become a champion barrel racer and earn her dad's approval. She'd accomplished one, realized she'd never have the other, and moved on. Once she'd passed the bar, she'd narrowed her search for a new home to places as far off the professional rodeo circuit as she could find. Melbourne, with its growing need for family law specialists, fit the bill.

Mitch gestured toward a faint glow that rose above the distant town. "I've been here almost six years. And in the interest of full disclosure, I'm a single dad. Divorced. But my ex-wife has been out of the picture for a long time. So." He paused a beat. "How 'bout you?"

How about her?

For the past ten months, ever since she'd hung her shingle outside a converted house in the town's quaint business district, she'd been too busy for relationships, significant or otherwise. A home-school education meant college and law school had demanded every ounce of her concentration. On the rodeo circuit, she'd been the new girl in a different town every week. The locals hadn't exactly rolled out the welcome mat so, other than that summer, her love life had been practically nonexistent.

But on a warm August night after she'd aced a difficult performance, dredging up her entire history wasn't on her agenda. Especially not with a tall, handsome man standing at her elbow. She studied his face and rediscovered the tiny dip in his chin that she used to trace with her fingers.

They spent hours reminiscing before she asked, "What do you do in your free time?" She kept her voice light enough to disguise a deepening interest, adding, "Besides attending charity events."

"Between chauffeuring my daughter around and my work schedule, my spare time is at a premium... Why waste it?"

She couldn't agree more. As his arm slipped around her waist, Amanda stepped forward. Ever so softly, Mitch brushed his lips across hers. She sighed into his kiss, letting her eyes drift closed. The gentle pressure of his mouth stirred her hunger for more, and when his tongue swept against her lips, she opened to him.

Tasting the sweet punch they'd sipped, Amanda smiled without breaking contact. She rose on tiptoe, her hands languidly stroking Mitch's broad chest. In response, the teasing flutter of his kisses deepened.

She melted against him as music rose from the barn and floated in the air around them.

Amanda breathed in the heady blend of Mitch's aftershave mixed with the same indefinable something extra she'd noticed earlier. The strangest sensation of coming home filled her being. She gave herself over to the thrill of the moment, the press of Mitch's hands against her back. She skimmed her fingers over the rough embroidery of his shirt, then buried one hand in his hair. Desire tugged at her core, turning her breath so ragged she barely heard the band leader announce the final dance of the night.

Sounding as breathless as she felt, Mitch groaned and broke their kiss. He gazed into her upturned face.

"We need to put in an appearance," he murmured. The long fingers of one hand gently tucked an errant lock of her hair into her braid. "How 'bout we pick this up later?"

"Yeah," Amanda whispered. They weren't kids anymore, and she placed her hand in his outstretched one, content to follow the evening wherever it led.

By the time they stepped into the barn's spill of light, the crowd inside had thinned to several dozen couples who swayed to the slow strains of a country ballad. Wait staff circulated among the tables, collecting dishes and utensils. Last call had long since passed. Behind the bar, the bartender loaded boxes onto a dolly.

Eager to return to Mitch's embrace, Amanda moved toward the dance floor. At the sound of a familiar voice, her footsteps faltered.

"Hate to interrupt." A decked-out cowboy stepped from the shadows near the door. "We're pulling out at seven tomorrow. You need to be back from—" his eyebrows wiggled suggestively as he jerked a nod toward

Mitch "—from wherever you're headed, early enough to help with the horses and your gear."

"Uh-huh," Amanda said with an easy grin. "The same goes for you, Royce Jackson. Or did I not see you earlier surrounded by adoring fans?" Smothering a laugh, she turned to introduce one of the rodeo circuit's most renowned practical jokesters to Mitch.

Only Mitch wasn't smiling.

Gone was the adoring expression of the man who'd been kissing her only moments earlier. A stony look had taken its place. His hand relinquished its hold on hers, and his gaze dropped to the floor.

"Sorry. It's later than I realized. I have to go. Thanks for the dance, Mandy, and…" Mitch had the good grace to stumble over his words. "Well, good luck." He turned abruptly, strode across the barn and out the door without so much as a single glance over his shoulder.

"What was that all about?" Amanda stared after the man who was fast making a habit of abandoning her in drafty old barns.

Apparently, Mitch Goodwin hadn't changed as much as she'd thought since she'd seen him last. Well, she had. And this time she wouldn't shed any tears for Mr. Hot and Cold.

Chapter Two

Mitch's swift, take-no-prisoners pace down the wide corridor of the Moore Justice Center slowed at the sight of the woman seated outside Family Courtroom 2. He turned away, his gaze sweeping the bare concrete walls and heavily trafficked carpet before he dared take a second look at a pair of trim calves and firm thighs. His chest tightened. There was no mistaking those legs. It didn't matter if the last time he'd seen them they'd been encased in buckskin. He'd recognize them anywhere.

A silent oath escaped his lips as he glanced upward. Gone were the twin braids, replaced by a businesslike bun, but less than two weeks ago those honeyed strands had rested against his shoulder. Even though she leaned over paperwork now, her face hidden, he had no doubt.

The one woman he would've sworn had ridden out of his life forever was sitting on a wooden bench outside the very courtroom where he planned to argue the most important case of his life.

What is she doing here?

Mitch refused to believe she had just happened by. After five years with the state attorney's office, he'd learned there was no such thing as coincidence. Something, or someone, had led her here at precisely—he checked his watch—nine forty-seven on August 13. Before the bailiff summoned him, he had to discover the reason. He settled on a line of questioning and let his feet take him where they wanted—straight to her side.

"Mandy."

She looked up from the yellow legal pad in her lap, gray-green eyes widening.

"Mitch," she exclaimed. Her full lips curved into a surprised-to-see-you smile.

He didn't buy her act, not for a second. He was willing to bet good money she'd noted his arrival the instant he'd emerged from the stairwell. The same way he'd narrowed in on her presence. And in the seconds it took her to gather her paperwork and gracefully unfold a frame that barely came to his shoulder despite a pair of black stilettos, he wondered at the pretense.

She stuck out a hand. "Good to see you again."

A whiff of alluring fragrance stirred through the justice center's stale, cold air. The scent reminded him of green grass and daisies and how well she'd fitted into his arms while they'd danced. Without thinking, he rubbed the soft flesh between her thumb and forefinger. When her eyes darkened, he released her hand and gave himself a stern warning to keep his distance. No matter how much he might be attracted to her, a footloose rider on the rodeo circuit had no place in his life. Not anymore.

Yet here she was.

Has she been called to testify?

Mitch brushed a speck of lint from his lapel, wishing he could just as easily knock off the devil perched on his shoulder. Because only a certifiably evil spirit would bring his single indiscretion into the courtroom where his daughter's future was at stake. He should never have asked the rodeo performer to dance, never bent down to place his lips against hers, never tried to rekindle what they'd had as kids…but he had. He worried what that error would cost him.

"Mandy, we need to talk."

One golden eyebrow arched. "Amanda," she corrected as, across the hallway, heavy doors swung wide. "We will. But not now. I hear Judge Dobson is a stickler for starting on time. You already brushed the pole once. I'd hate to see him penalize you."

Mitch scoffed. "What are you talking about?" He understood her reference to the rodeo event, but he hadn't taken a wrong turn in the law since he'd decided to put criminals in jail instead of freeing them.

"From what I hear, Dobson is the only family court judge in the county who hasn't had dealings with you. He wasn't too happy about canceling his annual fly-fishing trip to the Carolinas in order to hear this case."

Her words thinned Mitch's smile and straightened his spine.

"That's privileged information," he said, wondering what was going on, and determined not to let his confusion show.

"Yes." She nodded. "I suppose it is."

He tried not to watch as she bent to pick up a leather satchel. He lost that battle, though he won the war against letting her catch him. By the time she straightened, he was staring through a wall of plate glass overlooking acres of cattle pasture, as if he hadn't noticed the swivel of her softly rounded hips.

She didn't volunteer anything more and, wanting to maintain the air of control that served him so well in criminal court, he didn't ask. Their silence continued when she fell in beside him. Despite their difference in height, she matched him stride for stride, cutting across the crowded corridor the same way they'd cut a swath across the dance floor.

As they made their way down the courtroom's rows of churchlike pews, Mitch watched for her to peel off and take a seat among the witnesses and spectators. Instead, she kept pace until they reached the tables reserved for attorneys and their clients. Out of habit, he veered right. The misstep put him face-to-face with the woman he'd turned his back on before things could go too far.

Once more, she extended her hand. Once more, he wrapped it in his own.

"Amanda Markette," she said smoothly. "Attorney for the plaintiff."

"What is this, some kind of joke?" He stared at her, fighting a sudden urge to yank his fingers from her grip.

"Not at all, Mitch." Her tight smile vanished. Her eyes narrowed. "Your ex-wife hired me after her last attorney quit. I've been playing catch-up ever since, though I'm sure I faxed official notification to your office."

Mitch fought back a groan. Convinced he had right on his side, he hadn't paid much attention to his secretary's announcement that there'd been yet another change in his ex-wife's revolving door of representation. But peering over Amanda's shoulder, he spotted Karen at the plaintiff's table. He had to admit she appeared sedate, settled. In fact, casual observers might mistake her for any one of a thousand suburban housewives…unless they caught the malice-filled glare she aimed his way.

Summoning his best don't-give-a-damn expression, Mitch returned the favor, marshaling his thoughts as he took his place on the hard wooden chair at the defen-

dant's table. He snapped open the latches on his briefcase and dug out a raft of paperwork, flipping through
it until he reached the fax containing a name he'd have
recognized if he'd bothered to read it. Scanning quickly,
he noted credentials that exposed a glaring hole in his
ability to sum up a person's character with a single look,
a single kiss. Evidently, a lot more than Mandy's—
Amanda's, he corrected—appearance had changed
since the summer they'd spent together.

"All rise for the Honorable Jeffrey Dobson," the bailiff announced.

Standing, Mitch squared his shoulders.

With a rustle of black robes, a white-haired man
took his place behind the raised desk at the front of the
room. He nodded briefly to those in attendance. Wood
creaked and feet shuffled until everyone had settled
back into their chairs. Mitch's gut tightened as the bailiff read the petition for custody of Hailey. His mouth
went cotton-dry at the thought of losing his little girl.

"Counselors?" the judge asked.

At the other table, Amanda stood and gave her name.

"Ms. Markette," Judge Dobson murmured.

Then it was his turn. "Mitchell Goodwin for the defense, Your Honor."

The man seated on the dais adjusted rimless glasses
and draped a hand over his microphone. Blue eyes hard-
ening in an unsmiling face, Dobson stared down.

"You're familiar with the old adage that a lawyer who
represents himself has a fool for a client, aren't you?
You intend to be that fool, Mr. Goodwin?"

"Yes, Your Honor," Mitch snapped, though the only
thing he was truly certain about was the need to protect his daughter.

AMANDA CROSSED ONE leg over the other, shifting just enough to keep Mitch in her peripheral vision. Thank goodness she'd been sitting down when he'd stepped through the stairwell door. One peek at his carefully tousled hair and sculpted features, one whiff of his woodsy cologne, and the same weak, loose-limbed feeling that had practically been her undoing at the dance had flared again. She'd nearly succumbed to it that night. Probably would have if he hadn't suddenly abandoned her on the dance floor, leaving her with bruised lips and a crushed ego.

She eyed the man across the aisle and assured herself it wouldn't happen again. He might've broken her heart once upon a time, but she wasn't the kind of girl to chase someone who didn't want her. Especially when that someone was her client's ex-husband.

She guessed, in a way, she should thank him. That Sunday morning after she'd loaded all the gear and Brindle onto her dad's trailer, she'd gone straight to her office to prepare for her newest case. The moment she'd seen Mitch's name in her files, the second she'd discovered she would face him in court, her stomach had performed a set of acrobatics that had made her ride the night before look tame. If they'd actually spent the night together...

Well, *that* couldn't happen. She wouldn't let it.

Or so she'd sworn. Until just a few minutes ago, when all her nerve endings had tingled at Mitch's touch. She'd almost reconsidered the whole idea of representing his ex-wife, only now it wasn't just her heart at stake, but a child's well-being, too. Her client swore that Mitch's self-centered and career-driven attitude had destroyed their marriage and was taking its toll on their daughter.

Amanda resisted the urge to wince. She hated to think that the boy she'd loved and lost had grown into such a hard-hearted man, but if even half her client's claims were true... Well, a little girl was entitled to more than an absentee father, one who never had time for pillow fights or school plays.

Determined to do her best for the child, Amanda drew in a steadying breath. Her hands stopped trembling. She folded them neatly and forced her lips into their trademark half smile, the one she'd perfected during countless rodeo performances and a short stint as the nation's top barrel racer. As recently as ten days ago, her confident air had assured thousands that, no matter how dangerous the stunt, she had everything under control. That same expression came in handy whenever she wanted to impress a judge.

Or get under the skin of a particularly thorny opponent, like Mitch.

Her client stirred restlessly and tapped her long nails on the tabletop. Amanda gave the woman a warning glance while, at the front of the room, the judge sorted through paperwork associated with the case. Karen rolled a shoulder before whispering, "Do you think I'll be able to take Hailey home with me today?"

"I doubt if he'll rule on custody right away," Amanda answered. "If things go smoothly, though, we'll get you the visitation you deserve."

Even in family law, possession counted for something, and for the past four years Mitch Goodwin had had sole custody of his daughter. Judge Dobson might resent having to cancel his vacation to hear this case, but he wouldn't rip a healthy, reasonably well-adjusted child from the only home she'd ever known. Not without good reason. And the odds were against a seasoned attorney like the man at the other table committing an act so egregious it forced the judge's hand.

Eventually, Amanda intended to prove that Hailey was better off with the parent who could spend the most time with her. It might take months—such cases often did—but given that Mitch carried the heaviest caseload in the state attorney's office, she'd do it. She had only to prove how far he worked into the night— every night—leaving the care of his little girl to a parade of nannies and housekeepers, and the judge would rule in favor of her client.

Permanent custody and adequate child support was their long-term goal. Visitation, on the other hand, was practically an inalienable right. She'd lock that in today.

"You have to be patient. We'll start with an afternoon visit and go from there."

Karen sighed and flipped bottle-blond hair over one shoulder. The platinum color was popular among the nightclub set, but according to judicial insiders, Judge Dobson was quite the conservative. Amanda made a mental note to suggest a subtler shade before their next court appearance.

At the bench, the judge swept papers into a pile. He rapped their edges against the desk, the solid thunk sounding throughout the confined space.

"All right." His baritone voice drew everyone's attention.

Amanda gave Karen's hand an encouraging squeeze and faced forward.

"Having read the custody suit and the defendant's responses, I'd like to ask the plaintiff a few questions." He turned to Karen.

In rapid-fire succession, Judge Dobson ran through the list Amanda had expected. Karen answered just as they'd practiced. She expressed remorse over the breakup of her marriage, insisted Mitch had denied her every attempt at being a part of their daughter's life. Looking every inch the mother who'd been wrongfully stripped of her parental rights, she assured the court that she intended to make Brevard County her home. Bella Designs, the upscale dress shop where she worked, closed early enough that she'd be home before dinner. Her two-bedroom, furnished apartment wasn't the Ritz, but a social worker had approved it. She was even was saving for a house, a place with a yard her daughter would enjoy.

When she finished, the judge jotted down a few quick notes, letting everyone in the courtroom take a much-needed breath. Amanda reached beneath the table and patted her client's hand. Karen had given no indication that she was anything more or less than what she claimed to be—a woman who deserved to see her little girl, hold her in her arms and be her mommy. As long as nothing destroyed that image, their case was solid.

A glance at Mitch told her the man would try his best to undermine it. She didn't envy him. From the way Dobson's face hardened, her opposing counsel faced an uphill battle.

"Mr. Goodwin, your ex-wife appears to be making a new start under what must be trying circumstances. I think we can agree that, for whatever reason, she abandoned your marriage and her child. But that's in the past." Though Dobson's expression never changed, his voice softened. "Let's cut to the chase here. The plaintiff has reestablished herself in our community." Ticking off items one by one, he held up his fingers. "She has a job, an apartment and no arrest record. Although I'd like further time to monitor the situation, I see no reason to keep Ms. Goodwin from her daughter. Let's start with a forty-eight-hour visitation every other weekend. We'll meet back here in three months to see where things stand."

Karen gasped and started forward. Amanda restrained her.

"Not yet," she whispered. If she were sitting in Mitch's place, she'd have another argument up her sleeve. She watched the muscles in the lawyer's neck bunch into thick cords. His jaw clenched so tightly she wondered how he'd manage to get any words out.

"Your Hon—" Mitch stopped and cleared his throat. In a hoarse voice, he stated, "Your Honor, four years ago, when Karen walked out on our marriage, she left with our building contractor. Now, Ron faces embezzlement charges. Because of her association with known criminals—"

"Objection, Your Honor." Amanda was on her feet. "My client has no criminal record and there's no evidence that she—"

"Sustained." Dobson's fingers waved her into her chair. Any hint of compromise faded from his voice as he turned to Mitch. "Mr. Goodwin, your ex-wife's friends and associates are no more a matter before this court than yours are. You had to know before coming in here that the state of Florida has never completely refused visitation rights for a parent. I'm disinclined to buck that trend."

Karen had claimed Mitch possessed a violent streak. She'd even hinted that both she and Hailey had suffered from it. That was the only part of her story Amanda had refused to believe. Despite the fact that she'd seen Mitch react in anger—once—she couldn't accept that the boy she'd loved had grown abusive. She told herself prosecuting attorneys didn't rise to the top of the heap by losing control. Still, she'd checked around. No one had ever seen so much as a single hair rise on the back of Mitch's neck.

Judging from the waves of anger now rolling off the man, those who claimed Mitch Goodwin was incapable of losing his temper had been wrong. Railing against the family court system, he launched into an angry tirade. His strenuous objections echoed through the room.

Dobson lifted his gavel and rapped it sharply on the bench. A single tap was enough to stem Mitch's torrent of harsh words. The tall lawyer's expression grew shuttered, his eyes blank.

"I'm sorry, Your Honor," he stated.

Dobson gave him a hard look. "You should be. If you ever raise your voice in my courtroom again…"

Mitch never lifted his eyes. "Yes, Your Honor. It won't happen again, Your Honor."

"Court is adjourned." Dobson's gavel struck again and, with a flurry of black robes, the judge hustled into his chambers. Practically before those watching had surged to their feet, the door slammed in his wake.

"Well." Karen flounced back in her chair and pointed a finger at Mitch. "On TV, he'd go to jail for contempt."

"Real court is different." Amanda settled her hand over Karen's forcing down her client's outstretched arm. "We won more than we expected," she soothed in her most lawyerly voice. "Why don't you let me work out the details? That's what you pay me for."

Karen raked her manicured fingers through her hair. "Fine," she agreed, although her angry glare said she was anything but pleased. "As long as you remember that he stole my daughter—and my life—from me.

When we're done, I don't want him to ever see Hailey again. Have I made myself clear?"

This was a different side of the client who'd quietly slipped into her office two weeks earlier. Amanda reminded herself that emotions ran high in child custody cases. Karen wasn't the first parent to want revenge. But proving Mitch unfit even to see his daughter? The man might be coldhearted—he'd definitely been in the wrong in preventing Karen from seeing Hailey. But the courtroom was no place to extract vengeance. Truth be told, his objections and the judge's reaction to them were so vehement, Amanda almost felt sorry for Mitch.

She mustered a conciliatory expression, but by the time she swung around to face the man across the aisle, the door to the hallway was closing behind him.

Chapter Three

Halfway down the wide corridor, Mitch dropped his briefcase to the floor at his feet. He leaned back against the wall and concentrated on drawing strength from the hard concrete blocks. In five years as a prosecutor—no, longer than that. On the Law Review and at a thousand Sunday dinners where the senior partner of Goodwin & Sons dished out arguments along with the mashed potatoes, he'd never lost his cool the way he'd lost it in court this morning.

Mitch rubbed his temples, surprised his hands still shook with anger.

He was lucky Dobson hadn't cited him for contempt and locked him up overnight. Worse, the way things stood, the Suwannee River would freeze over before the judge ruled in his favor on the simplest of motions.

And that wouldn't protect Hailey.

The doors to the courtroom swung open. His ex-wife and her lawyer emerged. The sight of the two women chatting like old friends drove a spike right through the center of his gut. While Amanda guided her client into a waiting elevator, he studied the polished and astute woman who bore so little resemblance to the girl who'd worn T-shirts and shorts like a second skin. Even wearing an off-the-rack business suit, she outshone the sequined "Mandy" he'd waltzed around the Boots and Spurs barn.

She was good at her job, he'd give her that. She'd always had a competitive edge. After that summer, she'd used it to rise to the top in professional rodeo. But now she was putting it to work against him. And that only made him more determined to get back in charge of himself. He ran through possible scenarios for their upcoming conversation as she crossed the carpeted hall on three-inch heels that put an extra dash of sass in the swing of her hips.

"Hey, Mitch."

She'd lost her familiar smile, replaced it with a frown. He warned himself not to mistake her expression for concern.

"Amanda," he acknowledged.

"Looks like we have some things to sort out."

She settled against the wall beside him. Her face lifted into the sunlight streaming through banks of windows, and gave a small sigh. Her lashes drifted down until they lightly brushed the translucent skin beneath her eyes.

Mitch straightened and edged away. "The other night, why didn't you tell me you were an attorney?"

"We were at the bar association's fundraiser." Cat-like, Amanda continued to soak up the sun. "It wasn't obvious?"

"Not when you were racing across the arena astride a horse, it wasn't," Mitch grumbled. "I didn't see any other lawyers there dressed in leather and spurs."

Amanda faced him, the light turning her eyes more green than gray. "No, they'd all donned plaid shirts and denim. Definitely courtroom attire," she said drily. "But since you ask, I was in charge of entertainment.

I hadn't planned to perform—I gave that up years ago. But my dad skipped out at the last minute. I…" She scowled. "The show had to go on," she said, her jaw tight. "I filled in."

Mitch thought back to the quiet nights when he and Mandy had stayed up after all the other campers had turned in. Those days, her attitude toward her dad had been one part hero worship, two parts neglected kid. If Mitch was hearing her right, Tom Markette's image had lost its shine.

"Amazing performance," he conceded. Seeing her precariously balanced on one foot atop a thousand pounds of thundering horseflesh had stirred feelings he hadn't experienced in all the years since his marriage had crashed and burned. Later, when he'd held Mandy in his arms, swaying to country music, he'd wondered if the time was finally right to try again.

He swallowed hard and looked up to find Amanda staring at him. Keeping their conversation on track wasn't as easy as he'd expected. He struggled to regain his composure.

"Have you talked to Karen about our past? Or the stampede?"

Amanda made a derisive sound. "She knows."

"And she doesn't care?" Not that he'd believe *that* for a minute.

"Why should she? It's not as if we're involved. We knew each other as kids. The other night, we shared a couple of dances."

"We did a little more than dance."

"We kissed. Which you obviously didn't enjoy, because the next thing I knew, you'd left me standing in the middle of the floor with egg on my face."

She brushed her fingers across the lips he'd been crazy enough to devour.

"I owe you an apology for that," Mitch admitted. "The guy who spoke with us—"

"The pole bender. Royce."

Mitch nodded. "Yeah, that's the one. From what he said, I assumed you'd be heading out with them the next morning. It made me stop and think." He stopped now, not wanting to insult her by saying what was on his mind—that his days of getting involved with women who didn't stick around were over.

Beside him, Amanda stiffened. She leaned closer, her words a whisper no one could overhear. "Just so we're clear on a couple of things. One, I don't sleep with men I've just met. Even if we do have some kind of history. And two, not that it made any difference then or makes one now, I'm here to stay."

Mitch met her glare with raised eyebrows. She was right when she said it didn't matter. If timing was everything, theirs couldn't be worse. Amanda stood on the opposite side of the one issue that meant more to him than all the convictions he'd ever attained. Even if he were interested in a woman who could ride a horse at breakneck speeds and still feel meltingly soft in his arms—which he assured himself he wasn't—she represented his ex-wife and was, therefore, off-limits.

"Karen doesn't do anything without a plan. You don't think she picked you at random, do you?"

"Sorry to disappoint...." Amanda's expression said the joke was on him. "But, yeah. There just aren't that many family law specialists in town. Most of the others refused to take her case. Or they quit once they found out who they'd be up against. I was simply the last on the list. Besides," she added pointedly, "she signed me before the rodeo."

Amanda's brow furrowed. "You do know what they say about you, don't you? That you won't cut a deal, no matter what."

She made it sound like a bad thing, but his reputation was something he'd worked hard to achieve. He refused to apologize for it. "You didn't walk away," he pointed out. "What makes you so different?"

He could name several attributes that made her stand out from every woman he'd ever known, but that kind of knowledge wouldn't help him in court. And, if he was going to protect his daughter, he needed to know more about Amanda Markette than he'd known about her when they were teens.

She stretched her arms before folding them securely across her chest.

"I happen to believe my client has right on her side. Karen wants to be a part of Hailey's life. Every child needs their mother."

Mitch stifled a groan. Of course Amanda would feel that way. Her own mom had died the summer before rodeo camp. But Karen...well, Karen was a whole other ball game. "She doesn't want our daughter any more now than she did four years ago."

He'd thought long and hard about what had brought his ex-wife back into his life. Their marriage hadn't really had much chance to begin with. He'd done the honorable thing, marrying Karen after he'd gotten her pregnant, but she'd always been money hungry. She'd never understood why he wanted to prosecute criminals, not defend them. Or why he turned down his dad's annual offer to rejoin Goodwin & Sons and the membership in the swanky golf club that came with it.

Any hope for their marriage had died while their house was being built. She and their contractor, Ron, had accused him of nickel-and-diming it into mediocrity. A few months later, Karen had handed Mitch the keys to the front door, placed a squalling infant in his arms and climbed into Ron's SUV.

Now, with the builder in a serious financial jam, Karen was most likely looking for a new source of income. Mitch would bet his last dollar that's all their daughter meant to his ex-wife. And since Florida courts rarely awarded child support when the guardianship was shared, first she'd have to win sole custody. Something he'd do everything in his power to prevent.

He eyed the woman next to him and kept his insights to himself. There were things about her client Amanda would have to discover on her own. His job was to make sure Hailey didn't suffer in the process.

"You should know I intend to appeal Dobson's ruling."

"I expected no less. You won't succeed, but I understand why you have to try." A silky strand of hair had escaped Amanda's bun. She smoothed it into place. "In the meantime, you'll have to abide by the ruling."

"Whatever," Mitch growled through clenched teeth. "Let's work out the specifics. A week from Friday, where would your client like me to bring *my* daughter?"

He read the hesitation in Amanda's eyes. When she suggested it might be better if they met someplace neutral, such as her office, the ruse didn't fool him for a second.

"What don't you want me to see?" Certain she was hiding something behind her innocent expression, he sharpened his focus. "How bad is this place where she's living?"

"It could be better," Amanda admitted. "The social worker approved it but..."

"But their standards are lower than mine." His head throbbed and he rubbed a hand over his forehead. He lifted the lid on the potent mix of fear and anger that had simmered ever since he'd been served with papers on the custody suit.

"I'm holding you personally responsible for Hailey's safety. And now, if you don't mind, I have to go home and tell my four-year-old her mother is back in town and determined to ruin our lives."

He turned to leave, but Amanda's hand on his forearm stopped him. If he thought he'd read concern in her expression earlier, there was no mistaking the worry on her face now.

"She's just a little girl," she murmured. "Are you really going to drag her into this?"

The implication hurt more than Mitch cared to admit. "Of course not," he blustered. The bands across his chest tightened. "Give me some credit, will you? I will fight you with every fiber of my being, but I've never prejudiced Hailey against her mother. I won't start now. I'll present it as an adventure, a sleepover with her new best friend."

The words left a bitter taste in his mouth, and he walked away, the same way he'd walked away at the end of summer camp and again after the Saddle Up Stampede. Only this time, he didn't have the memory of soft kisses to sustain him.

ON FRIDAY AFTERNOON, Amanda shifted in her chair in the cozy seating area where built-in shelves housed hundreds of books on family law. "Are you ready for this?"

"You know Mitch and I can't be in the same room

without drawing blood." Karen's noisy exhalation sent coffee sloshing over the side of her cup.

Amanda handed across a napkin and said firmly, "You will." While her client blotted, she dredged up the tone she'd used whenever a horse had balked at a new trick. "For Hailey's sake, you'll be civil with each other."

And I'll keep my distance.

She had her own reasons for avoiding Mitch Goodwin. Though he would never make it onto her list of Mr. Possibilities, he'd managed to awaken feelings she didn't want to admit. It took effort to remind herself that a man with single-minded dedication to his career was not who she wanted in her life.

"Do you and Hailey have big plans for the weekend?" Deliberately, she switched subjects so her thoughts wouldn't drift toward the hot summer nights when she'd dreamed of sharing more than kisses with Mitch.

Karen smoothed the skirt of a dress Amanda recognized from last year's fashion magazines and sighed. "I wish I didn't have to work tomorrow. I'd really like to take Hailey to Disney World."

An uneasy feeling bloomed in Amanda's chest. Cautiously, she asked, "What will she do while you're at the store?"

"Why, come with me, of course. She can hang out in the employee lounge, watch TV."

The answer triggered memories of all the scary, lonely nights Amanda had spent in their trailer while her parents performed to the roar of a crowded stadium. Her own years in arenas where disaster was only a loose stirrup away helped her maintain her composure. "I don't think you should take your daughter to work."

Karen's brows arrowed down over her eyes. "I don't see why not."

"I'm thinking safety issues. It was hard enough to childproof your apartment."

Amanda bent forward, setting her glass of soda on the serving tray. She thought she'd made it clear that the visitation rights they'd won in court could be ripped out from under them if Hailey got hurt. But one glimpse of Karen's blank expression and Amanda knew she needed to try again.

"Think of all the dangers in the back of the store. Coffeepots within reach. Needles and scissors. What if Hailey walks out the door while you're busy with a customer and wanders down the sidewalk?"

"Well, I hadn't thought of that." Karen rummaged through her trendy little purse until she pulled out a sleek cell phone. She thumbed the device and glanced at the screen. "You know," she said, resettling the expensive bag at her side, "it's just not fair that Mitch can afford to give our daughter anything he wants when I can't."

The lament was becoming so familiar, Amanda couldn't ignore it. She stared openly at her client, willing the woman to understand that money wasn't the determining factor in whether or not someone made a good parent. Sure, a man like Mitch, with his high-octane career, could provide for his daughter financially, but at what cost? The little girl spent most of her time with a housekeeper. What children really needed was their parents' time and attention. That was something Karen *could* provide.

"Okay, okay," the blonde huffed at last. "I'll take the day off. I don't know how I'll make my rent at the end of the month if I can't work on Saturdays, but I'll do it if I have to."

"I'm sure it's the right thing—"

When their talk was interrupted by a loud knock, Karen's cup chattered against her saucer. "Is that Hailey?" She placed the coffee she'd barely touched on the table.

"Right on time." Amanda doused her own shiver of anticipation. Summoning her usual smile, she asked, "Are you ready?"

Though her client licked her lips, she didn't budge. "Could you let them in? I'm so nervous, I don't think I can stand."

"Are you sure?" Amanda hesitated. The court-appointed psychiatrist had urged Karen to be the first to greet her daughter. But considering how the shaky woman held one of the sofa pillows in a stranglehold, there wasn't much chance of that happening. And there wasn't time to talk her through it. Not with Mitch and Hailey waiting in the hallway.

"Okay, then." Amanda took a steadying breath and crossed the room.

At the door, she steered clear of Mitch's intensely brooding eyes and firm lips. It was harder to ignore his towering presence, but she sent her gaze skimming past his white button-down and over a pair of long legs to the little girl who stood quietly at his side.

It wasn't every day Amanda had the chance to reunite a mother with her child. The occasion ranked high on a list of achievements that included earning a gold buckle at nationals, passing the bar exam, winning her first case. She smiled broadly.

Just as she did, Hailey Goodwin tipped her head away from scrutiny of patent leather Mary Janes that peeked from beneath her navy pinafore. The ribbons at the ends of her thick plaits of black hair fluttered. Her dark blue eyes widened in an elfish face, and her rose-bud lips parted to form a deep oval.

"Mommy?"

Stunned, Amanda stumbled back a half step. For an instant, she saw herself curled in a deep chair reading books with a child on her lap. She caught a glimpse of them in a kitchen, baking cookies, doing all the things mothers and daughters were supposed to do. The image was so powerful she almost regretted the large, male hand that dropped to Hailey's shoulder.

"No, honey," Mitch said, breaking the spell. "This is Ms. Amanda, a friend of ours. Your mom is here, though. Isn't she?"

In the second it took Amanda to regain her composure, she silenced the useless ringing of her biological clock. Some people should not have children, and having practically raised herself, she'd decided long ago she would never pass her parents' mistakes on to another generation. She liked kids, though, and mustering up an added dose of excitement for this one, she bent down until she was on Hailey's level.

"Your daddy's right. I'm a friend of your mom's. She's waiting for you. She's *so* excited to see you."

Tiny lips quivered. "Where?"

"She's sitting on the couch. Would you like to come inside and see her?"

The girl's fingers slipped into Amanda's, but with each step into the room, Hailey's progress slowed. They'd barely cleared the threshold before the child's eyes brimmed with tears.

Puzzled, Amanda cocked her head. "What's the matter, sweetie?" she asked.

A mix of consternation and joy warred on Hailey's features. Amanda looked to Mitch for help, but after one glimpse of the pain that clouded his eyes, she looked away. Before she could come up with more than a few soothing words on her own, she sensed movement at her elbow and stepped aside.

"*I'm* your mama, honey." Arms widening, Karen sank to her knees before the child. "Come give me a hug."

Hailey glanced up at her father while Amanda held her breath and searched Mitch's face. He'd hidden the pain she'd seen only seconds earlier behind a look that was pure encouragement, but the child's owl-like gaze swung between her parents. She didn't move until Mitch leaned down and whispered in his daughter's ear. With his hand on her back, he guided the child into Karen's waiting arms. Silence reigned while Karen clung to her daughter. Long seconds passed before one of Hailey's thin arms crept around her mother's neck.

Amanda blotted her cheeks and risked another quick glance at Mitch. She wondered if he saw the rightness of the moment, but his eyes were shuttered. A tic in his jaw told her he was fighting his own emotional battles.

"You're such a big girl. So grown-up," Karen murmured after a few minutes. She swiped at her eyes and held the child at arm's length. "And so pretty."

"You have pretty hair, too." Hailey ran her fingers through her mother's platinum locks.

"Thanks, honey." Karen rose. She smiled down at the child. "We're going to have a good time this weekend, just the two of us." She took Hailey's hand in hers. Her voice cooled when she turned to Mitch. "I'll drop her off at the house at five o'clock on Sunday. Is there anything else I need to know before we leave?"

Mitch stared at the colorfully decorated, bright pink suitcase he'd dropped by the door. "I put a list in her bag. Her likes and dislikes, her favorite TV shows, a description of our bedtime routine—it's all in there."

"Oh, I'm sure we'll do just fine without all that." Karen patted her daughter's hand. "Won't we, Hailey?"

The little girl's gaze swung from her mother to her father and back again, while beside him, Amanda practically felt the temperature around Mitch rise. Hoping to keep everyone calm and moving in the right direction, she intervened.

"That was very thoughtful of you, Mitch." She aimed a pointed look toward her client. "I'm sure Karen appreciates it."

With Hailey's hand in hers, the woman moved toward the door. As she passed Mitch, the child wrenched free.

"I don't want to go, Daddy." Hailey clung to her father's leg.

Karen hadn't even slowed down. From the doorway, she called, "Hailey, be a good girl now, and let's go."

Mitch peeled his daughter's hands away from his leg and squatted down until he was even with her tearstained face.

"Shush, baby. It's all right. You're going to have a sleepover with Mommy tonight and tomorrow night. I'll see you on Sunday. We'll play together, same as always."

"But I want you to come, Daddy. I don't want to go alone." Hailey's lower lip trembled and she hiccuped.

"Daddy can't come this time, honey. But remember? We packed Mrs. Giggles in your suitcase." He looked up and addressed Karen directly for the first time. "Mrs. Giggles is her favorite doll. They sleep together every night." His focus shifted back to his daughter. "You be a good girl for Mommy now and have fun."

"Okay, Daddy, but I won't have fun," Hailey conceded. Her toes dragged with every step, but she crossed the carpet to her mother's side.

Karen immediately whisked the little girl into her arms. Within seconds, she had grabbed the suitcase and disappeared out the door. The sound of her heels tapping against the hardwood floor outside the office faded into the distance.

Mitch's posture sagged the minute the door swung closed. He turned to face Amanda. The mask he'd hidden his emotions behind slipped away, exposing a potent mix of anger and pain.

"I hope you're satisfied, Counselor," he said through clenched teeth.

She was. Time would prove her right, but there was nothing to be gained by pouring salt in the man's wounds. Instead, she strove to remain professional. "It's the right thing to do, Mitch. That little girl deserves to be with her mother…and her father."

His hand on the doorknob, he issued a stern warning. "I meant what I said about holding you personally responsible for Hailey's safety. Heaven help you if my daughter is harmed in any way."

And then he, too, was gone.

Amanda sank onto the chair behind her desk. To win this case she'd need all the help heaven could give— and more—now that the combative prosecuting attorney had shown his vulnerable side.

Chapter Four

At four-thirty on Sunday afternoon, Mitch conceded defeat. Without the sound of little-girl laughter bouncing off the walls, the house was so quiet he couldn't concentrate on the opening argument he'd present in the morning. In the past, he'd grumbled about the thousand-and-two interruptions Hailey insisted were absolutely necessary whenever he worked at home. He would never make that mistake again. Her tiny fingers on his keyboard or frequent breaks for make-believe tea parties were nothing compared to the worries that troubled him now.

Where was she? Was she happy? Was she hungry? Safe? Did she miss her dolls? Her toys?

The first time he'd looked into his infant daughter's face, he'd fallen for her cute little button nose. From that moment on, he'd made it his business to know exactly where she was and that she was taken care of every moment of every day. Relinquishing her into Karen's hands had required all the courage he possessed and then some. He'd walked out of Amanda's office Friday afternoon feeling as if someone had filled his heart with sand. Sand that had slowly dribbled through an hourglass, marking the time until his little girl would be home again.

He checked his watch. With another half-hour to go, he logged off, closed the laptop and moved to the window where he could stare in earnest at the empty spot in the driveway. Except it wasn't empty. He blinked, unable to believe that his ex-wife had returned their daughter ahead of schedule.

There was a flaw in his reasoning. The legs that swung out of the driver's seat of the Chevy Suburban were too curvy to be Karen's. Honing in on them, he decided Amanda looked even better in shorts now than she had as a teenager. He reminded himself that he wasn't interested. Only one thing mattered at this point, and he held his breath until Hailey bounded from the car.

The second his little bundle of sunshine hit the ground, he headed for the entry hall. He covered the distance in half the time it took her much shorter legs to make it across the front lawn. Still, he hung back, waiting as the doorbell sounded once, then twice, because she liked to hear the chimes echo through the house.

"Dad-deee!" she cried the minute he opened the door. She lunged for his legs.

When he'd played football in high school, two-hundred-pound linemen had struggled to bring him down. Today, forty pounds of little girl brought him to his knees in a heartbeat.

Hugging her close, he ran his hands through hair that smelled of perfume instead of the baby shampoo and talc he kept in Hailey's bath. His fingers tangled in a snarl, and he grimaced, wanting to wrap his protective arms around her and never let go. For her sake, he pried her away from him and rocked back on his heels.

"Look at you," he scolded, teasing. "I think you grew an inch while you were gone."

Pride danced in her eyes. "Mommy said I was all growed up and not her baby girl anymore."

Mitch fought the urge to roll his eyes. If Karen regretted missing out on her child's early years, she had only herself to blame. "You are growing up," he agreed, as Hailey snuggled in for another hug.

He shot a grateful look at Amanda.

"C'mon in," he said. The first week of September in central Florida still meant ninety-degree heat and the kind of high humidity best endured in short bursts while moving from one air-conditioned place to another.

"All in one piece, Counselor?" Amanda's smile was light and breezy. She placed Hailey's child-size suitcase on the floor.

"As far as I can tell," Mitch grumbled. "How'd it go?"

Amanda shrugged. "There were a couple of kinks, but nothing Karen couldn't handle. Things will go more smoothly next time."

Mitch suppressed a chuckle. His daughter could be headstrong and demanding when she didn't get her way.

Hailey backed out of his embrace to frame his cheeks with her little fingers. A frown pursed her lips. "Daddy," she demanded, "why did you make Mommy go away?"

Mitch stared straight into her troubled eyes. "I didn't, honey."

Her sneakered foot stomped the entryway floor. "Mommy said you did."

Mitch forced himself to exhale slowly. This was exactly the sort of thing he'd been afraid of. He'd never said anything bad about his ex-wife—not when his daughter was within earshot—and he refused to start now. "Remember when Nana came to visit?" he asked. "You wanted her to stay forever, but she had to go to her own home. Mommy has her own home, too."

If Karen had been standing in the doorway, he'd have clarified the rules, made certain she understood that using their child as a pawn in some sort of power play was both cruel and unnecessary. But his ex-wife hadn't dropped the child off. Amanda had. Why was that?

"Karen was low on gas," Amanda volunteered. "Your home is quite a drive from her apartment. It's lovely, by the way—your house." Tentatively, she sniffed the air. "Something smells good in here."

"Sga-betti," he said, pronouncing the dish the way his daughter insisted. "It's Hailey's favorite." Even he had to admit the house smelled a little like an Italian restaurant. Unable to sleep, he'd minced onions and garlic before dawn. The sauce had been simmering ever since. With nothing better to do, he'd prepared their salads— a large one for him, two or three bites of lettuce and a slice of cucumber for her.

"I still make the bread. Right, Daddy?" Hailey asked.

"Absolutely." Later, after he cooked the pasta and dinner was almost ready, she'd help him spread butter on the bread before he ran it under the broiler.

"So," Amanda said, her hand on the door, "a week from Friday, then. My office?"

"That works." He rose to his feet. Should he ask her to stay for dinner? If she spent some time with them, would Amanda see how wrong it was to rip Hailey from the only home, the only parent, she'd ever known?

He gave the idea a second thought before rejecting it. From the day he and Karen brought Hailey home from the hospital, Sundays had been reserved for friends and family. After their marriage broke up, he'd made it the housekeeper's day off, and continued the tradition. No meetings, no work intruded. Now, with Hailey spending every other weekend with her mother, he was loathe to share what little remained of their time together. Even for a chance to prove he was the better parent.

"We haven't thanked Ms. Amanda for bringing you home. What do you say, Hailey?"

"I want to play with my dolls, Daddy. Mommy didn't have any at her house. Just Mrs. Giggles." She planted her feet and leaned back, tugging on his hand.

Life was simpler when he let his daughter lead the way, but they'd been working on manners for the past few months. Sensing this was a good time to practice them, he hoisted her onto his hip. "Let's say goodbye now, and you can play until dinnertime."

Hailey buried her face in his neck. A muffled "'Bye," came from somewhere near his collar.

Good enough, Mitch thought. As he closed the door behind Amanda's retreating figure, Hailey whispered in his ear.

"Daddy, do I hav'ta go to Mommy's again? I like it at my house. Can't she come here? I want to stay with you."

Mitch swallowed. Balancing his own wants and concerns against the judge's orders was going to take more out of him than he'd imagined. "I know, honey. I want you to stay with me, too, but we have to share some time with Mommy. Did you have fun with her this weekend?"

"No," Hailey insisted. "I don't like her 'partment. It smells bad. Mommy's TV doesn't get Baby Einstein."

"We'll make sure to pack your DVD player next time so you can take your favorite videos," Mitch soothed. His heart broke a bit as he explained to his daughter that even wonderful little girls didn't always get what they wanted. He struggled, trying not to let Hailey sense his pain, trying to make light of a difficult situation. "You'll go to Mommy's again, but not for two whole weeks."

After that, there'd be only four more visits before his next court date. By then, he'd find a way to change Judge Dobson's mind.

"I don't want to!"

When Hailey's feet began to swing, he let her slide to the floor.

"I don't want to go!" In less time than it took him to put on his tie in the mornings, her voice sharpened into a shrill whine. "I don't want to. No!" She pushed against his legs.

She was winding up for a meltdown. And no wonder, after all the excitement and upset she'd endured over the past few days. Knowing a change of scenery sometimes headed off a temper tantrum, he suggested, "How about if we go to the playground?"

Hailey's chin jutted out. Sullenly, she asked, "Will all my friends be there?"

He checked his watch. There was still plenty of time to burn off some energy before it got too dark, but at this hour on a weekend they might have the park to themselves.

"Maybe one or two," he answered. "You like the big slide. And the swing set." They had their own in the backyard, of course, but Hailey enjoyed their trips to the pocket park where oak trees provided shade and the slides were longer.

She brightened at the idea. Her pink capris and matching top were casual enough to play in, so they left her suitcase where it was. Mitch turned the heat under the spaghetti sauce to the lowest setting before he exchanged his polo for a T-shirt. Sunblock was next, followed by mosquito spray for both of them. And in fifteen minutes, they were on their way.

From a distance came the steady roar of a lawn mower. Music drifted from a backyard, accompanied by the heady odor of barbecue. At the playground, Hailey darted past the basketball court where a couple of teens practiced their hoop shots. Spotting two of her friends, she made a beeline for the sandbox. The girls chatted for a few minutes before the trio headed to the jungle gym, a multilevel affair with intricate walkways and two sets of monkey bars—one for little kids, another for older children. The higher bars were off-limits, and while Mitch tried not to hover, he kept a close eye on his daughter, just in case she decided to test the rules.

Soon laughter filled the air as the girls raced up and down the ladders and slides, darted in and out of a small playhouse and tried to see who could go the highest on the swings.

Sweat and humidity quickly plastered Hailey's hair to her scalp, and he wished he'd thought to bring her headband. He dug in his pockets until he found an elastic, and beckoned. As his four-year-old climbed down from jungle gym, a car pulled to the curb and a slim, well-dressed woman stepped out.

"Hey, Hailey. Hey, Mitch," called the president of the homeowners association. She waved and picked her way down the mulched path, stopping to pull a dandelion out by its roots.

"Lydia." He barely glanced up from the task of corralling loose, damp hair into a lopsided ponytail. "There you go," he said, and watched his daughter scamper back to the play set.

"Are you coming to the HOA meeting this Friday?

We're trying to get that house over on Redbud repainted. The owners used the wrong shade."

"Sorry. I'll be in court all week." Which was just as well. He tried to avoid the association's somewhat petty politics. What did it matter if the painters used periwinkle instead of robin egg? Blue was blue, wasn't it?

Lydia might be a little too Stepford Wife for his taste, but she knew their community better than anyone. While Mitch kept a close eye on Hailey, he learned who had landed new jobs and which houses were going on the market. Ten minutes later, Lydia glanced at her watch.

"Time for dinner," she noted. "Emma, Reese, let's go. Good talking to you, Mitch." Her girls sped toward the car. "Gotta run."

"Time for us to head for home, too," he answered. But when he glanced over to the swings, all he saw was an empty seat rocking back and forth. His stomach sank and he hurried toward the monkey bars.

How Hailey had scrambled to the top of the highest set in the two seconds he'd taken his eyes off her, he didn't know, but there she was. His daring little girl sat atop the middle bar, her feet dangling.

"Hailey, we've talked about this," he said as firmly as he could. He moved into position beneath her. "Let's get you down from there."

She laughed at him. "Look, Daddy. I'm up high."

"I see that, Hailey, but you know the rules. You're not supposed to climb on those bars, not until you're older." Though he might be a pushover when it came to bedtimes, clothes or new toys, he didn't compromise where her safety was concerned.

"But, Dad-dee." Her legs moved up and down like pistons, her feet stomping the air.

Mitch, afraid she'd knock herself off her perch, grabbed for a foot. He missed, and her sneaker connected with his chin. Pain shot through his mouth and down his neck. For one brief second, he saw stars. "Ouch, Hailey." He rubbed his jaw, sure it'd be black-and-blue by morning.

"Great," he muttered. Walking into court looking as if he'd been in a brawl was just the image he needed. His voice dropped into the no-nonsense register.

"Hailey Jordan Goodwin, I want you down from there this instant."

"Yes, s—"

One second, the pride of his life was hanging on to the bars with both hands, the next she'd tipped over the side and was plunging headfirst to the ground eight feet below. With no time to think, Mitch reacted. As his daughter dropped in front of him, he grabbed whatever he could get his hands on. An arm, a leg, what did it matter as long as she didn't break her neck?

He managed to keep her from hitting the ground. Before he could breathe a sigh of relief, her screams knifed his gut.

"Daddy! It hurts! It hurts."

Fear crawled up his back and lodged in his throat. One part of him yelled, *Jump in the car. Rush to the nearest hospital.* Another part, the parental side, the side that had been through a dozen bumps and bruises that turned out to be nothing, insisted he hold her close. He hugged his sobbing daughter to his chest, wrapped his arms around her, didn't let her move.

"Let's let Daddy take a look," he said when her tears tapered off.

Gently, he stretched the neck of her shirt to one side. Nausea rolled in his stomach and he lost the ability to breathe at the knob of bone that stretched the skin off to one side of her shoulder.

Dislocated. He knew it without thinking. A similar injury his senior year had cost him a date with the homecoming queen and benched him for the rest of the football season.

He patted his back pocket and found nothing. An image of his cell phone surfaced. He hadn't bothered to grab it from the charging station when they left the house. Without moving, he signaled the boys on the basketball court. One of them hustled over.

Mitch forced himself to stay calm. Any movement could worsen the injury, so he couldn't carry Hailey home any more than he could drive to the hospital with her in his arms. "Do you have a phone? Can you dial 911. We need an ambulance."

"Hey, Joey, grab the cell out of my bag," called the pimply-faced kid. He craned his neck, probably hoping for gore.

In Mitch's arms, Hailey whimpered.

"Shh," he whispered. "It'll be all right. Daddy's got you. Everything'll be okay."

At the hospital, doctors and nurses hovered, treating Hailey with gentle hands while Mitch insisted on summoning the area's best orthopedist. Amid X-rays and a thousand questions, he fretted over whether or not to airlift his child to the large children's hospital sixty miles away. An overreaction, he knew, but nothing was too good for his little girl. In the end, he calmed at the specialist's assurance that the injury was a simple one. Though she'd have to keep her arm in a sling for six weeks, they could avoid surgery.

"I'll give her something to make her drowsy," the doctor said after Mitch agreed to the procedure. "It'll relax her enough to let me pop the bones back into place."

Mitch willed his hands to stop shaking. Hailey was being very brave and he told himself he should do the same. He ran a hand over his own bruised jaw, wishing he could trade his pain for hers.

"Can I stay with her?" he asked.

"Of course," the doctor replied. "It'll be good for her to see a familiar face before she drifts off. Don't worry, Dad. A lot of kids don't even remember the accident after they wake up."

At least that was something to be thankful for, Mitch thought when a nurse approached with a scary-looking needle. He felt himself blanch, but his daughter had used up all her tears and barely cried. Drowsily, she slumped against him. He thought he had a slim chance of coming out of the accident with his soul intact when Hailey turned to him and asked, "Daddy, why did you hurt my arm?"

An instrument clattered into a steel tray. The noise made him flinch.

"Sorry," murmured a nurse. Her back to him, she headed out the door.

"You fell, baby," Mitch reminded his child. "Daddy caught you before you hit your head, but your arm got hurt. The doctors are going to fix it, though, and you'll be just like new."

"Okay, Daddy." A tiny bubble formed at the corner of Hailey's mouth. "I'm sleepy."

And then she went out like the proverbial lightbulb. Seconds later, the doctor and nurse were at his side. They helped Mitch ease the sleeping child onto the exam table.

"I think you should step outside now."

The nurse scowled when he argued. The doctor remained firm—Mitch had to leave. He brushed a kiss across his daughter's forehead and followed directions through a door to the chairs in the waiting area.

The slowest hour of his life passed before he heard someone call, "Goodwin? Relatives of Hailey Goodwin?"

Mitch set aside last January's issue of *People* magazine and stood. His eyes narrowed at a redhead in a rumpled business suit. She strode toward him, a clipboard clutched against her chest. He stared, vaguely recognizing her from the home inspection she'd performed shortly after Karen had filed for custody.

"I'm Mitch Goodwin. Is Hailey all right?"

The woman flashed an official-looking badge. "Mr. Goodwin, do you remember me? I'm Sarah Magarity. With the Department of Children and Families. An allegation of child abuse has been raised regarding your daughter."

"What?" Shock punched Mitch straight in the stomach. "That's not possible. She fell. She fell from the monkey bars at the park. I caught her, but her shoulder popped out of joint."

"I'm sorry," the woman said. "But once the allegation has been raised, the law is very specific. I must take your daughter into custody."

Mitch knew the law. He'd prosecuted men and women, fathers and mothers, whose misdirected anger had harmed their children. As far as he was concerned, they could rot in jail for the rest of their miserable lives. He'd helped put several of them there. But he hadn't hurt Hailey. The thought was so ridiculous he could barely fathom it.

"Wait a minute. Wait a minute." He reached for his

wallet and brandished his own ID. "You know I'm with the state attorney's office. Surely we can talk about this."

"Mr. Goodwin, I'm sorry." Ms. Magarity shook her head. "The fact that you're an officer of the court actually works against you. We have to be doubly sure you didn't harm your daughter."

Mitch stared past the woman's shoulder to the door he'd walked through. A manned and locked door. One that stood between him and his child. Quickly, he weighed his options. Any outburst on his part would only make the situation worse.

"Get in touch with my ex-wife then," he growled, crossing his arms. "She lives at the Pineda Apartments on US 1." He rattled off the phone number he'd committed to memory.

Ms. Magarity's expression softened. "I've already called her. She's on her way. We'll take it from here, then. You might as well go home."

He wasn't the type to create a scene, but if the woman from DCF thought he'd blindly go along with her plan, Mitch had news for her. "Lady, you're crazy if you think I'm leaving here without knowing my daughter is okay."

Sarah shrugged. "Your choice, Mr. Goodwin. But I advise you to go home. There'll be an emergency hearing tomorrow. You need to be ready for it."

"So, you're in Arkansas, Dad?"

The phone braced against her ear, Amanda studied the contents of her refrigerator. A three-week-old apple, two cartons of yogurt and a package of ham were not the stuff rich Italian sauces were made of. Unable to replicate the delicious smells that had emanated from

Mitch's kitchen, she grabbed the milk jug, asking, "And next week you'll be where?"

"Tulsa. After that, Texas. Then maybe I'll swing by Melbourne. Visit for a while."

Yeah. Right.

Amanda poured a glass without bothering to reach for a pen or paper. Her dad's plans were as fickle as the weather. It was one of the things she'd disliked most about her childhood—never knowing if she'd wake up to find their motor home parked outside an arena in Lincoln or Tupelo. When she'd hung up her spurs and listed her goals for the future, "a house without wheels" had come right after "go to college" and "get my law degree."

And now he thought he could just stop in whenever he wanted? She certainly wouldn't welcome him with open arms. After he'd skipped out on the Saddle Up Stampede, she'd spent the weekend converting her guest room into storage space.

As expected, her dad had a veritable litany of excuses for why a trip to see his only child might not *actually* fit into his schedule. He followed those with the usual invitation for Amanda to chuck her mundane existence and join him on the road.

"I'm still holding out for a Markette father-and-daughter reunion tour."

"'Fraid not," Amanda answered. "The dust settled on my rodeo days a long time ago."

Thanks to him, she'd made one exception, and all it had brought her was trouble.

"Well then, I'll be seein' ya," he said, though they both knew he wouldn't.

"Keep your—" The phone made a clicking sound.

"Boots in the stirrups," Amanda muttered into dead air.

Nothing new.

She settled the phone on the cradle. Milk calmed her and she helped herself to a long swallow. She wandered into the room where she'd stored all the paraphernalia from her rodeo career. Sure, she had a few regrets. She missed the velvety soft muzzle of her horse, the exhilaration she felt after a good practice run, the smell of fresh hay. None of that was tempting enough to lure her away from the life she'd built.

And Mitch. How does he figure into your plans?

She worried her lip. The last thing she needed in her life was another man like her dad. Mitch had walked away from her twice already. Seeing him with his daughter this afternoon might have softened her heart just a smidgeon, but it didn't change the facts. She'd done her homework, talked to his coworkers, his neighbors. Everyone told the same story: Mitch was more committed to his job than his family. Thus, her attraction to the wickedly handsome lawyer had no more place in her future than another run at the top of professional rodeo or a starring role on the Markette Ropin' Team.

She straightened a photograph of herself in the crowded Las Vegas arena. In the picture, she was smiling and holding barrel racing's top prize aloft. Even then, she'd known she'd taken her last ride. Striding across the room, she closed the door on her past.

The phone rang again. Amanda finished her milk and almost let the call go to voice mail. A glance at the caller ID changed her mind. Before the headset cleared the cradle, she heard a woman's shrieks pour from the earpiece.

"I warned you something like this was going to happen. Why doesn't anyone ever listen to me? I need a ride to the hospital. How soon can you get here?"

"Karen, slow down. Take a breath," Amanda ordered. "Are you hurt?"

"No, it's not me. It's Hailey." Somehow, she managed to sound exasperated and afraid in the same breath. "Mitch hurt her. Broke her arm or something. She's in the hospital, and I'm supposed to be there right now."

Time slowed to a crawl. "He...what?" The milk in Amanda's stomach soured.

This simply didn't make sense. Less than four hours ago she'd dropped Hailey off with her dad. If there'd been a sign the man was anything but thrilled to have his daughter home, she'd missed it completely. Praying Karen had the facts wrong, Amanda wondered if she should have paid more attention to her client's claims about Mitch's temper.

"Who?" she asked. "Who called you? And what did they say?" This time, she did grab a pen and paper, certain they would come in handy.

"I don't know." Karen whined so forcefully Amanda could practically see the blonde shoving her hands through her hair. "Sandy or Susan. Somebody from family services."

Amanda ran through a short list of names. "Sarah Magarity from the Department of Children and Families? She did the home study to approve your apartment."

"Yeah, her. She said Hailey can't go back to Mitch's and there'd be a hearing. I don't know anything more. Just that I need to get to the hospital. You know I'm out of gas, and I don't get paid till next week."

Amanda glanced down at the shorts and T-shirt she'd

worn all day. A change of clothes was definitely in order. She'd make it a fast one. The art of stripping out of one costume while stepping into another was one of the few talents that had made the transition to her new life.

"I'll be there in fifteen minutes. Meet me outside. In the meantime, I'll make some calls and let you know what I find out."

By the time Karen climbed into the Suburban's passenger seat, Amanda had answers to some of their questions and a bad case of heartburn. She replayed what had transpired at the hospital and informed her client that Judge Dobson had agreed to an emergency hearing in his chambers. Hailey would spend the night on the orthopedics ward. She wasn't allowed visitors—at least, not until they all met with the judge. So instead of going to see her, Amanda steered her car toward the courthouse.

"But what does it all mean?" Karen asked. For once she wasn't wearing one of her designer outfits. Dressed simply in slacks and a pullover, the woman stared out the car window.

"It means you might get custody of your daughter a lot sooner than we expected."

Karen threaded her hands through her hair. "Full-time? That means Mitch'll have to pay child support, doesn't it? How much, do you think?"

The misplaced concern left a bitter taste in Amanda's mouth and she swallowed. "The important thing is Hailey's safety. If you don't take her, the judge will put her into foster care rather than risk another injury."

If Mitch had hurt his daughter.

To justify an emergency hearing, proof had to point its finger at the man who paced the corridor outside Judge Dobson's office. Though Mitch started toward them the second they stepped from the elevator, Amanda didn't dare meet his imploring look. She allowed herself only a single glance at his rumpled clothes and disheveled hair before she steeled her heart, draped her arm around Karen's shoulders and guided her client into the judge's chambers. She still didn't want to believe the man who'd held her in his arms could be capable of cruelty, but she'd worked with Sarah Magarity often enough to know the woman didn't make unfounded accusations.

Apparently Judge Dobson thought so, too. Once all the interested parties had gathered in his office, he ordered a restless Mitch to take a seat before turning to the young redhead. "This is your show, Ms. Magarity. Let's hear what you have to say."

Mitch leaped to his feet. "Your Honor, this is all a simple misunderstanding. I can clear it up if you'll just let me—"

The judge turned a flinty look on the man. "Nice outfit, Counselor," he said with a nod to Mitch's shorts and flip-flops.

In a move that was oddly self-conscious, Mitch smoothed a T-shirt that had seen better days. "I mean no disrespect, sir. I came here straight from the hospital. If you'll let me explain…"

"You'll have your turn, Mr. Goodwin," Dobson said drily. "Ms. Magarity?"

Glad she'd taken the time to change her own clothes, Amanda ran her hand over the linen slacks she'd grabbed from her closet. She gave Karen a tight smile and turned toward the thin woman, who'd chosen to stand by the windows rather than sit near either parent.

"According to Dr. Scarletta, the orthopedist called

in to treat Hailey Goodwin, the little girl and her father arrived by ambulance shortly after six this evening. Mr. Goodwin claimed the child fell from monkey bars at a playground. Just before Hailey was sedated, a nurse overheard the child ask why her father had hurt her."

Amanda sucked in a sharp breath. Kids—even well-supervised kids—got hurt. They did not accuse their parents of harming them. Her heart hammering, she waited to hear what else Sarah had to say.

"In compliance with the laws governing suspected child abuse or neglect, Dr. Scarletta immediately called DCF. I informed Mr. Goodwin that we were taking his daughter into protective custody pending an investigation and your ruling, Your Honor."

Loathing filled Dobson's eyes. "Seriously, Counselor? You hit your child?"

"No, Your Honor." Mitch sprang to his feet. "Karen was supposed to return Hailey at five. Instead, she had her attorney deliver my daughter home early. I had dinner almost ready, but I thought it might be good for Hailey to get outside for a while, so we went to the park. She…she climbed up on the monkey bars. I was right there beneath her when she fell. I caught her, barely. But she must have wrenched her arm or something 'cause…" He shook his head. His breath came in heaving sighs "Her shoulder popped and she screamed."

"Liar," muttered Karen.

Amanda fought a gasp and hushed her client as she exhaled.

"Did anyone see this accident, Mr. Goodwin?" asked Judge Dobson.

"I tried to explain all this to Ms. Magarity." Frustration laced Mitch's voice. "Hailey had been playing with two of her friends. Their mother, Lydia Crane, had stopped by to pick up her girls. A couple of boys were playing basketball not far from where we were. I asked one of them to call an ambulance."

Judge Dobson let his gaze drift purposely through the room. "None of them are here with you now."

"No, Your Honor. Until Ms. Magarity showed up at the hospital, I had no idea I'd have to defend myself tonight."

Dobson folded his hands across an ample stomach. "Yet you expect me to return this injured child into your custody? I don't think so." He stared openly at the man before him. "Mr. Goodwin, how'd you get that bruise on your cheek?"

Determined to keep her distance from the man who was wrong for her in so many ways she was beginning to lose count, Amanda had purposefully avoided looking directly at Mitch. The judge's words demanded she do exactly that. Now, staring at the fresh welt, one she was certain hadn't been there earlier in the day, she felt her heart sicken.

Mitch rubbed his reddened cheek. "She didn't mean to, but—" his head sank until his chin nearly touched his chest "—Hailey kicked me."

Amanda shuddered as she envisioned the little girl kicking Mitch in the face and the angry father yanking his child off the monkey bars. She let her gaze sweep over the room and saw reactions to the same image reflected in the other faces. Beside her, Karen flung herself back into her chair, her arms crossed, satisfaction glowing in her eyes.

At his desk, Judge Dobson glanced at the computer he'd booted up upon his arrival.

"We're already on the calendar for mid-November," he noted. He turned toward the social worker. "Ms.

Magarity, can you look into Mr. Goodwin's claims and complete your investigation in the next three months?"

Sarah looked up from the clipboard where she'd been jotting notes. "Yes, sir. I'm pretty sure we can."

Dobson nodded. "In that case, I'm placing the minor child, Hailey Goodwin, with her mother, Karen Goodwin, until the November hearing. If you can prove your case at that time, Mr. Goodwin, we'll revisit the custody issue."

Mitch stumbled back a step as if he'd been dealt a physical blow. "But, Your Honor, I—I didn't hurt my child. I would never..."

On the cusp of losing his daughter, he sent a fevered glance around the room. When he searched her face, sympathy stirred within Amanda at the plea for help she saw etched on his chiseled features. She fought the feeling with a quick reminder that, at the very least, Mitch had failed to adequately watch over his child.

Pain and betrayal flickered in the dark eyes he tore from hers, but the lawyer seemed to pull himself together. His shoulders straightened and he drew himself to his full height.

"What about visitation, Your Honor?" he asked. "By your own words, there's never been a case in the state of Florida where a parent's rights have been completely denied."

"You make a valid point." Dobson took his own survey of the room. "Visitation will be granted as long as it is convenient to the custodial parent. And supervised."

"You can't be serious," Mitch scoffed. "I'm not allowed to be alone with my own daughter?"

"That's exactly what I mean, Mr. Goodwin. And since I'm unwilling to add to the heavy load family services already carries, we'll need an officer of the court to ensure your daughter's safety. Ms. Markette, let's have you supervise all meetings between Hailey and her father. That all right with you, Counselor?"

Amanda's Mona Lisa smile failed her and she felt her lips part. As the person ultimately responsible for Hailey's safety, she'd be forced to spend hours each week in Mitch's company. One look at Judge Dobson's stern expression and she knew there was no point in arguing. For Hailey's sake, for her client's sake, she had no choice.

"Yes, Your Honor," she said. But, for the first time since she'd walked away from the arena, Amanda wondered if she should have stuck to barrel racing.

Chapter Five

Studiously avoiding so much as a glance in his direction, Amanda braced for another explosive protest from Mitch. When the only sound was the thunder of her own blood rushing in her ears, she risked a quick peek. The district attorney's dark-haired superstar slumped in his chair, defeat showing in every line on his weary face.

Amanda sharpened her gaze.

Was this some ploy to gain the judge's sympathy? Or hers?

She bit her lower lip, trying to figure out his game plan as a memory of Mitch as a dogged teen surfaced. At Camp Bridle Catch, he'd drawn calf roping for the summer-ending mini rodeo all the parents were invited to attend. At first, he'd been lucky if his rope went anywhere near the practice post. But he'd kept at it, breaking from the chute and throwing his lariat over and over. Long after the other campers and counselors had given up in disgust, he'd succeeded. She'd been so proud of him.

Now, eyeing him, she dealt with a host of emotions, but pride wasn't one of them. Mitch stood accused of neglecting his daughter. Or worse. No one would cut him a break until he proved his innocence beyond a shadow of a doubt. And neither would she.

But the man personified stubborn. He'd never agree to let her supervise his visits with his daughter unless… Unless he thought he could somehow maneuver around her.

If so, he was in for a big surprise. He wasn't the only one who had changed in their years apart.

A nudge at her elbow interrupted Amanda's attempts to anticipate Mitch's next step. As much as she wanted to brush it off, she couldn't ignore the frantic tugging on her sleeve that followed. She aimed a questioning look toward her client.

"The money," Karen mouthed.

Amanda glanced at the briefcase propped open on Judge Dobson's dark mahogany desk. From the way he shuffled papers, it was clear the man thought they'd covered enough ground for one night. Disabusing him of the notion might earn her a stiff reprimand and a position on his bad side, something she'd managed to avoid so far.

An insistent hiss accompanied another tug on her sleeve. "What about the money? How am I supposed to take care of Hailey if I have to work?"

She sighed. Karen's daughter deserved the kind of attention Amanda's own parents had never lavished on her. It was up to her to make that happen, no matter what the cost. She cleared her throat. "Your Honor?"

Dobson glanced up from a neat stack of papers. "Yes?"

"I know it's late and we'd all rather head for home than tackle another thorny issue, but…"

"Get on with it, Ms. Markette." Dobson's face settled into rigid lines.

"Your Honor, this unexpected change in custody has caught my client unprepared. We need to consider finances, as Ms. Goodwin's salary from Bella Designs covers little more than her bare necessities. I'd like to request the court to order Mr. Goodwin to provide reasonable child support."

Dobson swung his heavy head toward Karen. "Are you telling me that, without help, you can't afford to take care of your daughter?"

At Amanda's side, Karen stiffened. She met the judge's doubtful look head-on.

"Not unless you expect me to quit my job and apply for food stamps, and that's something I'd rather not do. Hailey attends the area's best preschool. An expensive one. Plus, she'll need before- and after-school care."

Amanda blinked back her surprise when Judge Dobson nodded in agreement.

"Very well, then." He gazed toward the man still slumped in his chair. "Mr. Goodwin, you'll continue paying tuition for the minor child. I'm assuming she attends day care now?"

Mitch barely lifted his head. "No, Your Honor. My housekeeper, Esmeralda Santos, watches Hailey from the time she gets off the bus until I get home from work."

Dobson pursed his lips. "Well, then, we'll have to make other arrangements. Ms. Magarity, can you give me a ballpark figure on day care these days?"

From the corner where she'd taken a seat, Sarah's quiet voice sliced through the air. "Anywhere from five hundred to a thousand a week."

"That's insane." Mitch's eyes widened. He looked around the room as if seeking support. No one lifted a finger. "I can't afford those costs. Not on a public servant's salary. I'd have to fire Esme. She depends on that income to support her own family."

"If you have a better solution, Counselor, we're all ears." Dobson's dry commentary made finding an alternative sound doubtful. "I think we all agree that it's not in anyone's interests for Ms. Goodwin to lose her job."

Mitch turned an imploring look toward Karen. "I don't suppose you'd let our daughter come home after school? Esme could watch her until you get off work and take Hailey to your apartment."

Sarah Magarity intervened. "DCF won't approve that plan. There's too great a risk that Mr. Goodwin would spend unsupervised time with his daughter."

"Well, Counselor. You've heard DCF's position. Any other ideas?"

Mitch ran a hand through his hair. Talking to himself, he mumbled, "I'd have to check with her, see if she'd do it. If the only alternative is to find a new job, I'm sure she'd agree. After all, she loves Hailey." Lifting his head, he scanned every face before zeroing in on Karen's. "So, what if I continued paying Esme's salary but she reported to work for you instead? Hailey would still have a familiar figure in her life, and it'd resolve your child care problems."

Amanda watched Karen smile and nod before Judge Dobson polled the room.

When no one raised an objection, he lifted the stack of papers from his desk and settled them into his briefcase. "It sounds as though we have a workable plan. All right then. Mr. Goodwin, I'm ordering you to pay child support in the amount of one hundred dollars per week. In addition, you'll continue paying your daughter's tuition at her current preschool, as well as Ms. Santos's salary."

Dobson closed his briefcase. "I need to stress, however, that this is only a temporary arrangement. We'll revisit the support issue when we determine permanent custody of Hailey Goodwin in November." Latches snapped shut. "I'll want to see everyone's financial statements in my office by the time I return from North Carolina." He flipped over a page on his desk calendar. "That will be in mid-October. Make it the fifteenth." He honed in on Mitch. "In the meantime, you're to have no unsupervised contact with your daughter."

Mitch bolted for the door the second the judge dismissed them with a rap of his gavel. Amanda and her client followed, their heels sending small echoes through the empty courthouse while Karen spoke on her cell phone. She snapped it closed as they reached the exit.

"You can take me home," she said.

"Not the hospital?" If Hailey were her little girl, Amanda would want to be at her bedside.

"I just spoke to the nurse. Hailey's sleeping. Because of the anesthesia, they don't expect her to wake before morning, so I might as well get some rest, too." Karen brushed a hand through her hair. "It's a good thing Bella's is closed on Mondays. I have a feeling tomorrow's going to be a bear."

"It won't be a picnic, that's for sure." Amanda pressed her lips together. In the long run, having Hailey move in with Karen was the best thing for mother and daughter, but the next few days meant big adjustments for both of them. Karen would need to be at the top of her game.

On their way to her apartment, Amanda sought the answer to a question that had been troubling her. "You don't mind having Esmeralda at your place?"

Karen ran her fingers down the pinched crease of her slacks before answering, her voice nonchalant. "Oh, Esme and I go way back. When Hailey was a baby, she doted on the child. I wasn't at all surprised to hear she still works for Mitch."

Amanda had intended to use his parade of nannies and housekeepers as one of the arguments in her bid for sole custody of Hailey. Apparently, it had no validity. "I wish I'd known that earlier," she muttered under her breath.

A straightforward custody case. That's what she'd expected when she'd agreed to represent Karen. But nothing was turning out the way she'd planned.

Dropping her client off at the curb, she headed back the way she'd come. Mitch wasn't allowed within ten feet of his daughter. And it appeared that Karen needed her beauty sleep. That left only her to be at Hailey's bedside when the four-year-old woke scared and confused in the morning.

A FOUL ODOR FILLED Mitch's nose before he made it halfway up the sidewalk. The smell sent a sharp kick of fear straight to his gut.

Wasn't losing his daughter enough? Would he lose his house, too?

Fighting the pain of one more sucker punch in a night filled with them, he wrenched open the front door. No blaring smoke detectors. No flames. Both good signs. Without stopping to turn on the lights, he shoved something heavy out of his path, dropped his keys onto the entry table and raced for the kitchen. He slapped at the wall switch. Light blazed into the room. Dark wisps drifted lazily from the pan he'd left simmering on the stove hours earlier.

He flinched away from the too-hot handle. Grabbed a pot holder. Snatched the saucepan from the burner.

Carted it to the sink. Clouds of noxious steam rose as water from the tap splattered against brown goo.

Mitch gave the pan a few minutes to cool before poking experimentally at the blackened crust. He frowned at baked-on crud that would require more elbow grease than he could muster. After draining the pan, he dropped it into a trash bag, which he hustled outside. As the bag thunked to the bottom of the garbage bin he shook his head, refusing to question a legal system that could destroy the stable, secure life he'd built with his daughter as easily as he'd tossed out a burned pot.

On his way back into the house he nearly stumbled over Hailey's suitcase. Mitch's throat tightened, but he knelt beside the colorful tote, determined to make sure his daughter had enough clean clothes for a—*please, Lord*—short visit. He flipped the latches. Inside the suitcase, Mrs. Giggles lay on top of a jumble of clothes and shoes.

The howl he'd managed to suppress until now escaped.

He lost track of time while pain and disillusionment shot through him. Finally, he rocked back on his heels, struggling for control.

"Hailey," he breathed. He had to concentrate on Hailey.

He couldn't let his emotions get the best of him. If they did, he knew they'd destroy the few things he had left in his life—his career, his health. Things he'd need when the court realized its mistake and sent his daughter home. He pushed his feelings back, stuffing them into an imaginary box.

Before he slammed the lid, he tossed his feelings for Amanda into the box, too. Sure, she was his ex-wife's lawyer, but they had a history. They'd once loved each other. For a brief second or two, he'd thought they might again. Because of that, he'd expected her to at least give him the benefit of the doubt. But she hadn't. Her betrayal added to his pain.

Steeling himself, he dumped Hailey's clothes in the washer, threw open the windows to air out the house and headed into the kitchen to scrub splatters from the stove. From there, a natural progression led him to clean the counters and floors while he worked his way through the logistics of proving he wasn't the kind of monster who would hurt his child. A million ideas buzzed through his head while he scrubbed and mopped. By the time the first set of headlights glowed briefly through the living room window as a neighbor headed into town, he'd come up with a plan.

First, he would enlist Lydia's help in finding the boys who'd been at the park. The woman knew everyone from the toddler down the street to the octogenarian who'd sold the former grazing pastures to developers. She'd point him in the right direction. Once he found the boys, he'd prove Judge Dobson and that woman from DCF wrong. And finally, he'd bring Hailey home.

While dawn crept over the horizon, he showered and laid out his clothes for the day. One glimpse of the dark shadow along his jaw and he opted to forgo a shave. Straightening his tie, he considered requesting a delay in the court date against a small-time drug pusher. In the end, he decided not to. The best thing—for him, and for Hailey—was to maintain as much of their everyday lives as possible. That meant going to work even when his heart wasn't in it.

At Lydia's house, the smell of fresh coffee and warm syrup drifted through the screen door, a reminder that he hadn't had anything to eat or drink since lunch the day before. His mouth watered and he rubbed his stomach. Food would have to wait. He was a man on a mission, and that mission was to bring his daughter home.

"Lydia?" he called into the shadowy recesses of the kitchen.

"Mitch?" Leather soles slapped against tile. A slim figure appeared in the doorway. "Goodness, Mitch, it's not even eight o'clock. Is everything all right?"

He hesitated, taking a second to reconsider how much of the disastrous events he wanted to tell the neighborhood gossip. Surely Lydia didn't need to know his daughter had been taken from him or that he'd been accused of harming her. Not when he had every confidence he'd be able to clear his name and get this mess ironed out in time to have her back in her own bed before everyone headed home after work.

"Hailey's in the hospital. She fell from the monkey bars right after you and the girls left the park last night."

Lydia's eyes widened. "Oh goodness, Mitch. Is she okay?" Motioning him inside, she swung the screened door open.

"Her shoulder dislocated, but they were able to reset it without surgery. The doctor—Scarletta—swears she'll be fine." As for himself, he might never recall the injury without feeling sick to his stomach.

Lydia brightened. "He's the best in the area. Everybody uses him." Concern filled the look she sent over her shoulder to the kitchen table, where Emma and Reese had finished the last of their pancakes. "Girls, Hailey's in the hospital. We'll have to make cards for her this afternoon."

Her announcement started a clamor that didn't calm down until long after Lydia had used the accident as a lesson to teach her own children the perils of breaking the rules.

"Go upstairs now," she said, just when Mitch was certain he'd grind his teeth into pulp if she didn't let him get to the point. "Wash your face and hands, and brush your teeth. We don't want to be late." She aimed a sad smile his way. "Today's my day for the car pool, but I have a few minutes. I'm so glad to hear Hailey'll be okay. I just can't imagine… Oh, where are my manners?" she asked, when she finally stopped chattering long enough to draw a breath. "Can I get you anything? A cup of coffee? Is there anything I can do?"

Mitch ran a hand over his face. "I wouldn't mind a cup. It's been a long night."

"You must've been beside yourself." Lydia settled a mug on a place mat. She scooted the sugar bowl across the table and gave him a once-over. A crease formed between her brows as she searched his face. "You need some ice for that bruise?"

Mitch rubbed his jaw. So much for his hope that no one would notice. "Nah, it's all right. I got clipped by one of Hailey's shoes," he said without giving details. Or answering questions about his daughter he wanted to avoid. Questions that would only lead in a direction he didn't want to go.

"Ouch. So, what can I do for you?" Lydia slid onto the chair at the opposite end of the table. "Are you considering filing a suit? Because I can tell you, that park belongs to the county. Not the homeowners association."

"Relax." He swept a hand through the air. "The idea of suing never crossed my mind. Although I wouldn't complain if those high bars disappeared." He arched one brow pointedly.

"I'll make some phone calls. Whisper the right words

in a few ears. Trust me, it'll all be taken care of by the time Hailey's ready to play in the park again."

From the firm set of Lydia's jaw, Mitch had every confidence the woman would do whatever she set her mind to. A tiny chip of the weight he carried fell from his shoulders. He took a deep breath and dived into the heart of the matter.

"There's something else you can help me with. Did you notice the two boys on the basketball court yesterday?"

"Now that you mention it, I did see them," Lydia said. Her eyes narrowed. "They didn't have anything to do with Hailey's fall, did they?"

"No. One of them—his friend called him Joey—phoned the ambulance, since I'd left my cell at the house." The few sips of coffee he'd taken rolled uneasily in his stomach. "I didn't get the other one's name, but I'd sure like to find them. I was hoping you knew them."

The bangles on Lydia's wrist jingled as she moved. The cheery notes grated on Mitch's nerves.

"Sorry." Lydia checked her watch. "I didn't really pay too much attention. You know the way kids gossip, though. Eventually, I'm sure we'll hear all about it." She stood and walked over to the staircase. "Girls, five minutes."

"Almost ready!"

The sweet voices floated down from the second floor, reassuring their mom, but making it hard for Mitch to breathe. How long would it be before he heard Hailey's voice echo through their house again? What if it never happened?

He swallowed. Determined to take whatever steps were necessary to bring his daughter home where she

belonged—no matter how much it hurt his reputation—
he put the mug of coffee on the table.

"Lydia, I can't afford to wait. I need to get in touch
with those kids now. They have to come forward and
tell the authorities I didn't hurt my daughter."

"What?" An odd look crossed Lydia's face before
her usual composure settled into place over it. Her full
attention focused on him now, she strode quickly to his
side. "What's going on?"

Mitch sighed. Much as he didn't want to tell her the
rest, there was no way around it if he was going to get
her help.

"Somehow, DCF got involved. An allegation of child
abuse was raised. They're threatening to take Hailey
away from me."

"Oh, every parent's nightmare," Lydia whispered.
She shook herself. "Of course, that's ridiculous. I know
you, Mitch. You've been nothing but a devoted father.
If there's anything I can do—write a letter, speak on
your behalf, anything…"

"Thanks. I appreciate that. But finding those boys
is my best hope."

"Let me check with a few people." Lydia frowned
and fussed with her nails. "Do you know Cheryl Johnson? She lives two streets over. Her nephews live in
Tampa, but they come here to surf quite often. I'll check
and see if they were in town this weekend."

Despite the coffee he'd swallowed, Mitch's stomach
felt hollow. Tampa was three hours away.

"You think you could call her now?"

But Lydia was already shaking her head. "Cheryl
works the seven-to-three shift at the Space Center. I
won't be able to reach her until late this afternoon." Her

voice went soft as footsteps sounded on the staircase. "I'll call you later and let you know what I find out."

His neighbor raised a finger to her lips. "Thanks for stopping by, Mitch. Give my best to Hailey." Her voice dropped to a whisper as she propelled him to the door. "And don't worry. I won't tell anyone more than I absolutely have to."

Moments later, Mitch spotted Esmeralda's car parked at the curb outside his house. With part one of his plan to get Hailey home temporarily stalled, bringing the housekeeper up to speed moved to the top of his list. He hurried inside, where he broke the news of Hailey's accident as gently as possible.

"Things aren't going well with the custody case," he admitted. "And now, with Hailey getting hurt, the judge said she needs to live with her mother for a while."

Quickly, he explained the arrangement he'd worked out, reassuring the housekeeper that the situation was only temporary. Esme considered her options briefly while Mitch held his breath. Once she agreed, he did his best to ease the transition by giving her the day off. As soon as she headed out, he grabbed the suitcase he'd repacked in the wee hours of the morning, along with a large tote practically overflowing with Hailey's favorite toys, her DVD player, movies. On top of the pile lay Mrs. Giggles. Mitch loaded them all into the car and tried to overlook the way his hands were shaking by the time he finished.

Twenty minutes later, he pulled into an empty parking lot. He settled back to wait, needing to get his head straight before he spoke with the woman who had once been the girl of his dreams. He'd seen the censure and disbelief in her eyes last night. How she, of all people, could think he'd ever harm his daughter was beyond him. But there it was. She did. It was up to him to convince her otherwise.

AMANDA RUBBED HER BLURRY, sleep-deprived eyes. Though her vision cleared, the unmistakable shape of Mitch Goodwin remained bathed in early-morning sunlight. Much as she hated to admit it, the man did wonders for a business suit. His jacket hung from shoulders so wide they cast a shadow over a good-size stretch of earth. She couldn't see his trim waist, but thanks to a light breeze, his legs were a different story. The fabric of his slacks molded to them, outlining every muscle and stirring a very unadversarial warmth through her midsection.

What was Mitch doing outside her office? He couldn't possibly think he had the right to show up whenever he felt like it, could he?

Apparently he did.

By the time she put her car in Park and turned off the engine, he hovered just beyond her door. Amanda closed her eyes and reached for the one image guaranteed to strengthen her resolve against having anything to do with him. She pictured the little girl she'd spent the night sitting beside. The one whose small figure had been dwarfed by the huge bed, her tiny arm swathed in ACE bandages. Hailey had spent a comfortable night and was scheduled for release before noon. She'd slept until Karen arrived shortly before breakfast. Amanda was glad for that, but it didn't change a thing where she and Mitch were concerned.

She was an officer of the court. Mitch's ex-wife's attorney. And the one assigned to oversee any contact he had with his daughter. She wasn't going to cut him any slack just because they'd danced together a few weeks ago or spent one summer thinking they were in love.

Her lips thinned. Her shoulders firmed. Filled with new resolve, she grabbed her briefcase from the seat beside her and opened her car door. Her resolution faced its first test when Mitch invaded her personal space.

"Amanda. I thought Hailey might need these."

For the first time, she noticed the suitcase at Mitch's feet and the overstuffed shopping bag hanging from his fingers. Her eyes lingered on the items. Bringing his daughter's clothes and favorite toys was something only a caring, concerned father would do. But that didn't make a difference.

The man had been accused of harming his child. Whether he was guilty or not, it was her job to make sure Hailey was safe.

She hit a button and the liftgate on the Suburban rose. "You can put them in there." She gestured toward the storage area behind the seats. "I'll make sure Karen gets them."

Once the items were stowed, Amanda pulled herself erect and, brandishing her briefcase like a shield, aimed her feet toward the property she'd spent three months and the last of her savings turning into a law office. She crossed her fingers, hoping that would be the end of it, praying that Mitch, having delivered Hailey's suitcase, would get in his car and drive away.

She should have known better.

As a teen he'd been the very definition of persistence. That was *before* he'd grown into an adult who was used to having people do what he wanted, when he wanted. The man didn't give up easily. He fell into step beside her.

"Amanda, hold up a minute." His voice was uncom-

fortably close to her shoulder. "You know me. You have
to know I didn't do this. You know I'd never hurt anyone."

The trouble was, she didn't.

"You punched your brother. You hurt *him*."

"Kid stuff. Brother stuff. It happened ages ago."
Though Mitch's voice sounded dismissive, his footsteps faltered.

For a few seconds, Amanda let herself believe she'd
won the round, that the man who had cost her more than
one night's sleep would leave. But no, he'd only slowed
long enough to pull his cell phone from his pocket and
check the screen. At the door, she juggled her briefcase
and purse, inserting the key in the lock, then breezing
in to turn off the burglar alarm. When she started down
the hall, Mitch was right on her heels.

He waited until they were in her office before he
spoke again. "I've never in my life raised a hand to
anyone except my brother. And I've *never* struck my
daughter. Not in anger. Not for any reason."

"If that's true, why is Hailey in the hospital? Why
is your face bruised? And why were you banned from
seeing her? Why?"

A horrified look dropped over Mitch's handsome
features. "I understood when you didn't speak up for
me last night. You are Karen's attorney, after all. But
seriously? You honestly think I hurt my daughter?" He
squinted against the sunlight that poured through wide
window slats.

Amanda sighed. It wasn't up to her to believe him or
not. For that, she had to trust Judge Dobson and Sarah
Magarity. How things progressed from this point forward, however, *was* up to her. Mitch, obviously, needed
to understand the ground rules.

"I know you can't see her unless I'm in the same room."

"For now." His chiseled features turned hard and unyielding. "With or without your help, I intend to track down the two witnesses from the park. Once they explain I did nothing wrong, I'll have Hailey back home by the end of the week."

Okay, so apparently he hadn't been listening when Judge Dobson announced his travel plans. After all that had transpired last night, she could understand how Mitch might have missed a detail or two toward the end of what had been a tumultuous evening. Then again, maybe he'd been too busy checking his cell phone. She watched in disbelief as he retrieved it and glanced at the screen again now.

"Seeing as Dobson left for the mountains this morning and won't be back until mid-October, I wouldn't count on it."

Mitch looked up from the phone. His lips parted. "That's two months from now. There has to be some way around him. Another judge to fill in? Something?"

"'Fraid not." The situation was out of her hands. Even if the family court docket hadn't already been straining at the seams, Dobson was the only judge in the county willing to handle proceedings against the D.A.'s right-hand man.

She watched as the reality of the situation dawned on Mitch. His shoulders rounded. His head hung. His hand, the one holding the phone, dropped to his side. On the screen, a digital clock counted down the seconds until nine. He thumbed a button and the screen went dark. He spun away from her, striding to the windows.

A full minute passed before his strangled voice whispered through the room. "In that case, we need to arrange a schedule." His fingers danced over the keys on his phone. "I want to see Hailey as soon as possible. Tonight."

"Whoa, Counselor." Amanda held up one hand. Like it or not, Judge Dobson had put her in charge. She wasn't about to start off by letting Mitch dictate when and how they'd handle visitation. "We'll do this on my schedule, not yours. Which means during normal business hours." She flipped through the pages of her desk calendar. "Wednesday at ten is my earliest opening."

When Mitch gave his cell phone another glance, Amanda fought the urge to rip the device from his grip and hurl it across the room. Clearly, the man's priorities were a complete mess if he was more interested in watching the clock than arranging time with his daughter.

"Am I keeping you from something?" She didn't bother to tamp down the sarcasm.

"As a matter of fact, I'm scheduled to be at the courthouse in twenty minutes. Dobson isn't the only stickler for punctuality." The edges of Mitch's perfect lips tightened. "Wednesday morning won't work." He ground out each word. "Hailey will be in school."

Amanda nodded, conceding he had a point. It was important to retain as much of Hailey's normal schedule as possible. "Okay, we'll meet after school." She flipped to the next page. "What about Thursday afternoon?"

When Mitch turned the date down, explaining he'd be in court, Amanda eyed him tightly.

"Are you in trial?"

He nodded. "Back-to-back cases all week."

Despite her best efforts, she couldn't help feeling a little in awe of a guy who could focus on his job after having his life ripped apart. She weighed a hastily narrowing set of options. Between meetings with clients and her own appearances in family court, her days started at nine and lasted until well past a young child's bedtime. "Looks like Sunday afternoon is our only option. If Karen agrees, we'll meet here from two until six."

"Noon to five. At my house." Mitch's gaze swept floor-to-ceiling bookshelves and the small seating area. "There's nothing for us to do here except sit and stare at each other."

Amanda crossed her arms. "There's a playroom down the hall. Books, games, a TV. A small refrigerator for snacks. You'll meet there. From two until six. It's that or nothing."

Though she wasn't sure whether the granite in her voice or the clock tipped the scales in her favor, Mitch acquiesced to her demands. As he hurried from her office, she suspected the latter.

And wasn't that the heart of the custody case she'd prepared against him?

Amanda sighed. She'd grown up with career-driven parents. She knew what it was like to settle for dribs and drabs of their time, always vying to be good enough—or bad enough—to earn their attention. She wanted better for Hailey, for every child.

Mitch's work schedule overwhelmed his life. Even now, when the most important thing in the world should have been arranging to see his daughter, the man was in a hurry to get to court. Not only did that make him poor parent material, it made him a terrible partner for someone determined to make home and family their number one priority.

Someone like her.

Where had that come from?

Amanda threaded her fingers through her hair. She wasn't looking for a husband. Or even interested in starting a relationship. If she were, it wouldn't be with Mitch Goodwin. She'd crossed his name off her list after the Saddle Up Stampede. Now that she'd been tasked with supervising his visits with Hailey, she had all the more reason to keep her distance from the confirmed workaholic, dreamy blue eyes or not.

Chapter Six

"Where's my daddy?" Hailey clutched a bedraggled doll to her chest. Tears ran down the little girl's cheeks and her head swung from side to side, the motion sending her tangled hair flying. Her arm escaped the sling around her neck and, using her freed hand, she brushed dark strands from her face. Her feet drummed the floor. "Where is he?" she demanded.

"He'll be here, honey," Amanda soothed.

How was she supposed to tell Hailey that Mitch was late? Late for the all-important first visit with the daughter he hadn't seen in a week. The man might claim to love his little girl more than life itself, but his actions said otherwise.

Small wonder the child was upset. It didn't seem as if either parent cared enough to spend time with her. In her rush to enjoy a few hours of freedom, Karen had dumped Hailey in Amanda's care and sped out of the parking lot.

Poor kid. Amanda knew how she felt—she'd spent her entire childhood trying to earn *her* parents' love and affection. By the time she celebrated her tenth birthday with a cupcake she bought using her own allowance, she'd lost count of the nights she'd put herself to bed alone. Of all the meals she'd fixed once she was tall enough to reach the microwave. Of the fingernails she'd bitten to the quick trying to teach herself from the home-school manuals her mom tossed on the table. After the car accident, she'd tried everything to earn her dad's love and attention. Nothing had worked. Finally, she'd walked away, resolved never to pass that heritage on to another generation.

She swallowed, running a hand through curls Karen had loudly called impossible to tame.

"Come on, honey. Let me braid your hair. You want it to be pretty, don't you?"

Hailey's tears subsided. "Do you know how?" she asked, surveying Amanda with an expression far too skeptical for a four-year-old. "You look like a cowgirl."

The child's assessment was too perfect.

"You're right," Amanda said with a laugh. In boots and jeans, she didn't exactly fit the image of a hairstylist. Or a mother. No, she looked like she'd just come in from the barn. Which was exactly where she'd been.

"I do know a little something about hair, though." She shook out her ponytail. Just as quickly, she swept the strands off her neck and back into place. "Would you like to choose some rubber bands and clips?"

Hailey's head tilted. Her wary slant-eyed glance said she wasn't entirely convinced, but she nodded slowly.

Boot heels echoing off hardwood floors, Amanda retrieved a box of supplies from her desk drawer before leading the way into the playroom.

"Are you a real cowgirl?" Hailey asked as Amanda made swift work of knots and tangles.

"I used to be. Now I'm an attorney."

Hailey's breath caught. "Like my daddy?"

"We do different things, but yes, sort of like your

daddy." Amanda divided Hailey's hair into sections and began braiding. "And I still like horses."

Much as she hated to admit it, her dad had been right about one thing. Performing in the Saddle Up Stampede had rekindled her passion for riding. Though she would never appear professionally again—those days were over—she'd been out to Boots and Spurs several times in recent weeks. The ranch hands were glad to have experienced help in exercising a stable full of horses. Plus, riding helped her burn off tension, and after seeing Mitch again, she could use all the help she could get in that department.

She glanced down at his little girl. Now was definitely not the time to dwell on her disappointment and anger over Mitch Goodwin. Not with his daughter sitting at her feet. With an effort, she wrenched her thoughts away from the frustratingly handsome attorney and placed them firmly on entertaining Hailey.

While she shared a few of her rodeo adventures, the child listened in gape-mouthed silence. By the time braids trailed down her back and barrettes held wispy curls in place, Hailey's eyes shone like pennies. With Mitch still a no-show, Amanda suggested they watch a movie, and slipped *Black Beauty* into the DVD player. Instantly entranced, Hailey remained glued to the screen even when loud knocking resounded through the office nearly an hour later. She barely stirred when Amanda rose to answer.

At the door, Mitch attempted to barge past, wearing a distracted frown. "Sorry I'm late. I was on the phone with the district attorney and couldn't get away. Is Hailey in the playroom? How 'bout giving Karen a call. Tell her to come at seven."

Amanda grimaced. This was exactly the kind of

workaholic behavior she'd expected from Mitch. She eyed the man whose good looks and charm probably had women jumping through hoops at his every whim. Well, she wasn't one of them. It was time he learned a lesson or two, and after spending the last hour babysitting—no matter how sweet the child—she was in just the right mood to school him.

"Hailey's watching a movie. She'll be all right while you and I get a few things straightened out. Two o'clock means two o'clock," Amanda said, dispensing with the preliminaries. "If I have to give up my Sunday afternoons for you, the least you can do is show up on time. And Karen will be here at six, exactly as we agreed."

Mitch's eyebrows rose. "We can't make an adjustment? Just this once? I thought…"

"Whatever you thought, you were wrong. Sarah Magarity sent over a list of instructions I have to follow."

She'd hoped to review the rules with Mitch before Hailey arrived. Thanks to him, that hadn't happened. Now, the clock would tick away more of his visit while they hashed things out.

"Once we set a time, we have to stick with it. No last-minute changes."

A worried frown creased Mitch's mouth. "What else?"

Amanda inhaled deeply and tackled the biggest item on the list. "You can't question her about her arm."

Mitch's response was instantaneous. "What? That can't be right."

"I'm afraid it is. DCF wants to make sure you don't coach your daughter. If you so much as mention the fall, I have to file a report. So the, uh, incident, her shoulder, the trip to the hospital—it's all off-limits."

"I can't even ask if her arm hurts?" Mitch's blue eyes widened in disbelief. "What kind of father wouldn't at least do that?"

Hailey hadn't complained, not once. "Her shoulder is fine. She doesn't seem to have any lingering effects. Not as far as I can tell." Amanda considered the way the child had slipped her sling off and on. "I think your biggest challenge will be making sure she doesn't overdo it until the arm is fully healed."

Mitch studied the floor at his feet. "More trouble is the last thing I need, but…" He blew out a breath so deep Amanda caught the faint odor of mint. His lips thinned. "I won't mention it unless Hailey does."

His penetrating stare begged Amanda to believe him. After giving herself a quick reminder that she was there to observe, not judge, she cleared her throat. "Then I guess we'd better go see her."

But if Mitch planned to impress her with his child-rearing skills, he struck out with his next turn at bat. Instead of the greeting he obviously expected, his daughter gave him the silent treatment, staring at the TV as if her life depended on it. She even resisted his hugs, leaning out around his shoulder to see the screen.

According to what Amanda had read about raising a child—and ever since settling on family law, she'd devoured books on the subject—Hailey was simply punishing her dad the best way she knew how. Which didn't make it any easier for Mitch. For a moment, Amanda thought she saw tears in the big man's eyes. She turned away, not wanting to see his pain or consider the kind of father who'd be hurt by his daughter's brush-off.

Firming her own resolve, she crossed to a corner, where she'd left a court case she intended to review. As she settled herself behind a small desk, she half expected Mitch to berate his child or, at the very least, insist that she talk to him. Amanda braced herself, prepared to intervene if need be. But Mitch surprised her, settling on the couch beside Hailey, one arm draped over the seat back.

"Sweetheart, I'm turning the TV off now," he said when the movie ended, and less than an hour of their visit remained. A smile wreathed his face. "I brought the cups and saucers so we can have a tea party like we do at home. Will you help set things up?"

Hailey shrugged her shoulder and winced. "You do it, Daddy. My arm hurts."

Amanda cast a warning glance in Mitch's direction. He ducked his head as if to say she didn't have to worry—he wasn't going to break the rules. Apparently satisfied that his daughter was speaking to him again, he bent and straightened the sling around Hailey's neck.

"Let's use this, okay? It'll help your arm get better. There," he said, when her fingers dangled just beyond the edges of the blue cloth. "Now, how about some chocolate milk and cookies for our tea party?" He began pulling items from a tote bag.

Though she tried to focus on her reading material, Amanda paused to watch Mitch arrange fragile china on the low coffee table. Seeing the way he worked with Hailey stirred the faintest doubt about the accusations against him. Quickly, she blinked and looked away, reminding herself she was there only to observe.

Once everything was ready, Mitch draped a fringed towel over one arm.

"Your tea awaits, madam." He bowed slightly to his daughter.

Hailey giggled while he guided her to the place of

honor at the "head" of the table, where her laughter faded.

"Daddy, you didn't set a place for Miss Amanda."

Mitch's tone turned decidedly neutral. "I think Miss Amanda might be busy. She might not have time to have tea with us today."

"Sure she does, Daddy." Hailey's little face darkened. "I want her to come to my party."

Mitch lifted his hands, questioning. His imploring eyes found Amanda's and refused to leave them. "Would you? We have plenty to share."

She wavered. According to the rules, she wasn't supposed to interact with Hailey and her dad. Not supposed to interfere unless she thought the child was in danger. But when Hailey scampered across the room to stand at her knees and ask politely that she join them, Amanda realized she was nearly as susceptible to the little girl's charms as her father was.

The next hour passed quickly while the three of them sat at the small table, nibbled on cookies and drank make-believe tea. Mitch told stale knock-knock jokes that sent Hailey into gales of giggles. Once she warmed up, the little girl turned into a chatterbox, practically giving a blow-by-blow account of every minute she'd spent in preschool that week, and with Esmeralda.

Mitch soaked in the details like a man who might pull the memory of this golden hour out again and again, while Amanda struggled to remain objective. His rapt attention to his daughter dented her image of Mitch as a demanding workaholic. And by the time they'd eaten the last cookie and drained the last cup, the question of whether or not someone had made a terrible mistake troubled her thoughts.

All too soon, a horn sounded from the parking lot.

Glad for the interruption that put an end to her questions, Amanda brushed crumbs from her hands. "It's time to go now, Hailey. This has been fun, hasn't it?"

The little girl's eyes widened. "I'm not done." She grabbed her empty teacup, lifted it to her lips and made slurping sounds.

"Your mama's here to take you home, Hailey. I'm afraid you'll have to go," Mitch said, though anyone could tell his heart wasn't in it.

"But I didn't tell you 'bout my letters. I'm learning them at school, Daddy." Her little-girl voice shifted into overdrive. "*A* is for apple. *B* is for basket. *C* is for cat. *D* is for..."

Amanda glanced at Mitch. No help there. The man hung on his daughter's every word. Deciding she had to be the one to take charge, she stood.

"I'll get your doll—Mrs. Giggles, right?—while you say goodbye."

Her last word threw Hailey's emotional switch. Every trace of the sweet little girl who'd spent the last hour laughing and telling stories disappeared. Tears filled her eyes. Her mouth trembled.

"But I don't want to go to Mama's 'partment," Hailey protested. "I want to go to *my* house." The child scrambled to her feet and practically threw herself onto Mitch's lap. "Please, Daddy, please. Please take me home with you."

Mitch clutched his daughter to his chest. With one hand, he patted circles on her back while he whispered words Amanda felt sure he hated.

"It's all right, baby. I'll see you next Sunday. We'll meet right here, and next time I'll bring Chutes and Ladders. Would you like that?"

"Noooo!" Hailey wailed. Her voice rose higher. "Noooo! I don't want to go."

Mitch struggled to his feet, his daughter in his arms. Tenderly, he placed her on the floor and knelt down until they were face-to-face. "I don't like this any more than you do, Hailey, but you have to go home with Mommy now."

Tears rained down Hailey's cheeks. She threw herself at him, her arms going around his neck in a death grip, the empty sling shoved aside.

"Please, Daddy. Please let me come home. I'll be good, Daddy. I promise. I will. I'll be a good girl. Don't you love me anymore, Daddy?" Her sobs took up every inch of space in the room.

Outside, the horn blew again, longer this time, a signal that Karen had grown impatient. Amanda wondered if she'd be forced to literally pry the child out of her father's arms. The prospect was so unappealing that she waited while Mitch continued to murmur reassurances without giving in to Hailey's demands.

Without warning, the little girl changed tactics. "I *hate* you!" she screamed. She pushed at his chest. "I hate you! I hate you! I hate you!"

Helpless in the face of his daughter's tantrum, Mitch simply knelt where he was and clutched Hailey to him while her tiny fists beat a tattoo against his shoulders. Still screaming, she wrenched herself free and raced for the door.

Amanda caught up with the child halfway down the hall, where she cast a glance over her shoulder at Mitch.

The man stood, stricken, his face pale, his eyes wide, his expression one of utter desolation and vulnerability.

Hoisting Hailey into her arms, Amanda spun on one

heel and turned away. Mitch's pain was too heavy a burden to carry, his love for his daughter something she couldn't bear to see.

IN THE MIDDLE OF THE playroom, Mitch gripped the back of the couch for support. Legs spread, he let his weight fall forward onto his hands. He drew in heaving breaths, one after another, until he could think of his daughter's meltdown without wanting to curl into a ball in the corner of the room. Not that this was the first time she'd ever thrown a temper tantrum. Far from it. But there was no denying this episode had been in a class all its own.

"I'll be good, Daddy...I'll be a good girl. Don't you love me anymore?"

With his legs too shaky to support his weight, he rounded the couch and sank down on it, then buried his face in his hands. A thousand questions swirled through his mind as he tried to get a grip on Hailey's outburst. Did his sweet, adorable little girl honestly think she was to blame? That if she behaved better, she'd be able to come home again? Did she think he'd stopped loving her? Or that any of this was her fault?

He was still sitting there ten minutes later when the door at the main entrance opened and closed. Lifting his head, he listened to the clatter of boots in the hallway. His throat tightened.

Hailey's meltdown had been bad enough, but to have Amanda witness it only made things worse. He mopped his face with both hands, struggling to look strong when his whole world was falling apart.

"Is she okay?" he asked when Amanda stepped into the room.

In a strangely thready voice, she replied, "Hailey was winding down by the time I put her in the car."

"Yeah." He nodded. "She usually puts so much energy into her temper tantrums that she's exhausted by the end." If they were home, he'd hold Hailey in his arms and rock her, soothing hurt feelings with quiet reassurances of how much he loved her, how much he believed in her, until she fell asleep. By the time she woke to the familiar sounds and smells of her own bed in her own room in her own house, whatever had triggered the meltdown would be forgotten, faded into a distant memory.

But they weren't home. And, God help him, it didn't look as if they would be in the foreseeable future.

"How are you doing?"

"Been better," Mitch admitted. He tried not to read too much into the hand Amanda placed on his shoulder. He'd hoped to use their visitation to prove to her he wasn't the kind of father who would hurt his child. He'd wanted her to see the easygoing relationship he had with his daughter. To demonstrate why it was right that Hailey live with him and not her mother. After today's fiasco, he guessed he could kiss goodbye to those hopes. "Sorry you had to see that."

"I'm not."

The unexpected sympathy brought his head up. He searched Amanda's face, reading guilt in the sheepish look he found on her pert features. "Really?"

"It gave me a new respect for parenthood. The books make it sound so easy, but it's a tough job, isn't it?"

"Hardest thing I've ever done," Mitch answered honestly. "Till now." He took a deep breath, his decision made. "I should probably tell you that I can't let things go on this way."

Amanda's hand dropped from his shoulder. Her boots sounded against the wooden floor as she came around the couch to face him. Concern filled her eyes. "You're not going to do something stupid, are you?"

"Probably." The half-hearted grin he'd managed fell from his lips. "Hailey has to know she's not at fault here. I don't know where she got the idea, but she's decided she's being punished for getting hurt, and that's why she can't come home. You heard her—she said she'd be a good girl, that she'd behave. That kind of thinking can have a lasting impression."

In his job as a prosecutor he'd dealt with more than his fair share of women—and men—who'd followed issues with poor self-esteem right down the rabbit hole into poor decisions about education, relationships, crime. He didn't want that for his daughter. No way. "I don't like where this could lead."

Amanda planted one fist on her waist. "The fall is off-limits. If you so much as mention it, you could lose the right to see her altogether."

"I'm putting more on the line than you know." Unable to sit any longer, Mitch got up and paced the room, the conversation that had delayed his arrival spilling unchecked.

"Randall Hill's been tapped for a cabinet post. He'll do well in Tallahassee. The question is, who will replace him as D.A.? A week ago, I was the obvious choice. It's the job I've worked for ever since I became a prosecutor. This custody mess, though…" He shook his head. "It's a deal breaker, one I never saw coming."

He turned to face Amanda, not bothering to hide the emotional toll his decision had taken. "I'll risk it all for Hailey's sake, though. I can't let her go on blaming herself."

Beyond the windowpanes, Sunday evening traffic moved on New Haven Avenue. Inside the playroom Amanda simply stood for a moment looking at him. At last she took a breath.

"And I can't let you destroy your career. Or throw away any chance of ever getting your daughter back. I won't go into whatever did or didn't happen on that playground, but let me talk to her."

Mitch struggled to keep his jaw from dropping. "You'd do that?"

"Not for you," she said, though he had to have figured into the equation. "For Hailey. Right now, she thinks you don't love her. I've been where she is. I've lived through it with my dad. I still am. The thing is, it's different with you. You really care about her."

Mitch stared, hope and regret warring within him. One summer, he'd walked away from Amanda, leaving her to shoulder the blame for their breakup. Though he'd explained his actions, he'd never really apologized for them. That was something he could take care of, and there was no time like right now to do it.

"I'm sorry." When questions flashed in her green eyes, he continued. "After rodeo camp that summer, I should never have left things the way I did."

The firm line of her mouth shifted into a melancholy smile. "Thanks for that, but what happened between us...I got over it a long time ago."

"All the same," Mitch said, "I could have tried harder to get in touch, to explain why I left you hanging."

Amanda turned pensive. "I thought, once your parents and your brother showed up, you'd lost interest. That a rodeo gal wasn't worth more than a summer fling."

Her words pierced another hole in a heart that already felt as if it was peppered with buckshot. "No, never that. I was just young and stupid."

"We should split the difference and call it even," she offered. "After all, I was on the road eleven months out of the year. It would have been easier for me to phone you."

Knowing how much the concession cost her, Mitch took the olive branch. "Sounds like we were both waiting for a call that never came."

"Maybe we were," she said, her voice wistful.

Fighting a wave of nostalgia for what might have been, Mitch eyed the petite blonde. Despite the years and miles between them, he'd never been able to scrub her completely from his thoughts. If he crossed the room and swept her into his arms, could they regain the past that had been stolen from them?

He hesitated. The day had already contained enough emotional upheaval. Certain it was time to lighten the mood, he sent her an appreciative glance. "Nice to see that some things never change. You always did look good in jeans."

Amanda patted her slim hips. "High metabolism, I guess." She wiggled her eyebrows playfully. "You don't look so bad yourself."

Tension eased from the room, and soon they were getting ready to put the day behind them. Amanda began gathering the few toys his daughter had scattered about. Mitch pitched in, stacking dirty cups and saucers on a plastic tray. By the time he returned from the kitchenette down the hall, the dishes in his basket washed and dried, Amanda was loading the last of the toys into a built-in storage closet. He slipped the clean items into the tote bag along with the rest.

"Here." He held the tea set in his outstretched hand.

"You may as well store this in there, too. Looks like it might be a while before I'll need it at home."

The brush of Amanda's hand against his sent a low-voltage current straight up his arm and across his chest. He studied the inquiring eyes that turned his way, and knew she'd felt the same thing. Curls had fallen onto her forehead and he swept them to one side with his fingertips.

"Amanda?" he whispered.

Her cheeks flushed and her breathing changed.

As much as he hated to do it, Mitch told himself he had to draw back. The woman before him might have offered to intercede on his behalf with his daughter, but she didn't trust him, and without trust, neither of them could afford to give in to desire. Regretting every step, he forced himself to do the right thing.

"There's too much at stake," he whispered. "Hailey…"

"Right," Amanda agreed. Subtle changes in her posture told him she had come to her senses as quickly as he had. "You're absolutely right." Taking the bag from his arm, she spun around to place it in an empty space on the closet shelf. By the time she turned to face him again, her dreamy expression had faded.

Mitch knew there was only one thing he could do: leave her office. Determined not to make the same mistake he'd made before and simply walk away, he cleared his throat. Amanda peered up at him.

"Okay, then." She dusted off her hands. "We're agreed. I'll talk to Hailey as soon as possible. And we'll meet here at the same time next week?"

"Yeah. Only next time, I'll make sure nothing interferes with my schedule." Mitch stared down at Amanda, wanting to take her in his arms, knowing it was impossible. Should he say something? His throat dried up, forcing him to cough.

Amanda waved one hand in a sign of dismissal. "Well, if that's it, I guess it's time to go."

She seemed so self-confident that Mitch couldn't think of another excuse to stick around. He left then, though he wished things could be different between them. On his way out, he wondered if Amanda had buried the same thoughts beneath her poised exterior.

Chapter Seven

Traffic thundered along U.S. 1, not fifty yards from the doors of low-slung buildings with flat roofs. Amanda eyed the ramshackle apartments where boxy air conditioners wheezed ineffectively from windowsills. Behind them, the Indian River perfumed late-summer air with salt and the eggy smell of sea grass as water lapped at the edge of a sandspur-dappled lawn.

She pressed her lips together. A month had passed since Hailey had moved in with her mother. Had Karen started looking for a better place yet? Her little girl couldn't swim in the algae-tinted pool. The rusted swing set didn't look safe enough for a squirrel, much less an active four-year-old. Thinking a change sooner rather than later might be a good thing, Amanda stepped from her car and crossed the graveled parking lot to Karen's door.

It popped open before she had a chance to knock, and Hailey Goodwin gazed up at her.

"Mom!" the child called over one shoulder. "It's Miss Amanda. See ya later."

"Hold on a second." Karen emerged from one of the bedrooms, vigorously rubbing a towel through her wet hair. "Amanda and I need to talk."

When Hailey slumped into a chair, parked close to a

flickering television, Karen frowned. "You can watch TV now or go to the movies later. Not both."

"But Mom…" the little girl began.

Amanda held her breath, waiting to see who would win the test of wills.

"Hailey…"

Karen's no-nonsense tone and stern look turned the tide. Hailey reached for the remote. "'Kay." She sighed hugely as the screen went black. With Mrs. Giggles tucked under her good arm, the child headed toward the back of the apartment.

Amanda reined in her surprise. "That went pretty well. Are you two getting along better?" Frantic phone calls from Karen had been a nightly occurrence the first couple of weeks. Lately, they'd trickled down to a minimum.

"Those books on child development you lent me really helped," her client said with a shrug. "C'mon in." She gestured. "Coffee?"

"No, thanks." Soda was Amanda's preferred caffeine source, and she was saving her allotment for the afternoon. Carefully, she picked her way through the cramped living room. Beneath the usual clutter that went hand in hand with raising a child, the carpet looked freshly vacuumed. The stove in the tiny kitchen sparkled. "Looks like Esmeralda's been busy," she noted.

"She's been a godsend." Karen nodded. "I don't know what I'd do without her."

Amanda sank onto a chair opposite a stack of sales fliers. "Going shopping?" she asked while Karen poured herself a cup of dark coffee.

"Clipping coupons is more like it. The stipend I get from Mitch doesn't cover even half the cost of feeding a kid."

Amanda suppressed a sigh at the all-too-familiar complaint. People like Karen were the reason she worked on retainer, deducting her expenses from the money her clients paid in advance.

Karen twisted the towel around her hair, tucking up the loose strands with a practiced hand. She leaned back against the counter.

"And what are Mitch and my daughter doing today?"

"He wants to have a cookout. We're meeting at his house."

Karen batted eyes filled with questions. "Is that allowed?"

Amanda shrugged. Though she might be stretching the rules, DCF's instructions didn't specify where their visits took place, only that she be there to supervise.

"I thought it might be good for Hailey to see her own room, play with her own toys for a bit."

She didn't mention that she was looking forward to the change of scenery. Mitch was a master of excuses, each week finding fresh reasons to linger after Karen picked up Hailey. Amanda and he had spent hours together, talking, rediscovering the things that had drawn them to one another so many years ago. Lately, she'd caught herself thinking of him at random moments. Each time, she had to stop and remind herself of the reasons why a relationship with Mitch was a bad thing. One of those reasons sat across the table from her, and Amanda hauled her thoughts back to the present.

"You want me to pick up some more of her clothes while I'm there?"

"Hell, yes." Karen pointed to a mound of neatly folded clothes in a basket by the back door. "Seems like Esmeralda spends most of her time doing that child's laundry."

Karen brought her coffee to the table and pulled out the only other chair. "A cookout, huh? I can barely afford hot dogs, but I bet Mitch'll buy meat from Petty's Market. What I wouldn't give to have one of their marinated steaks." Her lips twisted in a wry grimace as she waved a hand at the coupons. "If I hadn't scored a couple of free tickets, I couldn't even afford to take Hailey to the movies this evening." She looked up. "Are you sure there's no chance Judge Dobson'll increase my child support?"

Amanda let her skepticism show in a raised eyebrow. With Mitch covering tuition, clothes and school supplies, as well as paying Esme to provide day care, Karen's sole additional expense was food. Which, unless Hailey had started shoveling it down when no one was watching, couldn't cost much.

"Judge Dobson won't be back from his vacation for several weeks. And I have to tell you that, based on my experience in family court, Mitch is already paying more than most judges would order."

Karen started to protest, but Amanda cut her off. It was time the woman faced the downside of child custody.

"Say Dobson awards you more money. There's bound to be a trade-off. You'd have to cover tuition or day care. That might leave you worse off than you are now."

"You're not just saying that, are you?" Karen's gaze dropped to the table and she sighed. "This isn't working out at all the way I expected. Don't get me wrong— things were over between Mitch and me long before we split up. But after Ron and I called it quits I thought maybe I could get some part of my old life back. I thought gaining custody of my daughter meant I'd be able to quit work and be a stay-at-home mom."

"That's a little unrealistic, don't you think?" Amanda felt a twinge of sympathy for her client and let her voice drop. "Until Hailey got hurt, Mitch held down a full-time job and still juggled child care and the responsibilities that went hand in hand with being a single dad." She took a breath. "Let's say you win permanent custody. Best case, you'll get only enough child support to cover Hailey's needs. Not yours."

"You're sure?" Karen must have seen the truth in her eyes, because her shoulders slumped visibly.

Amanda nodded. If Karen and Mitch were battling for custody in another state, maybe her client could hope for more. But not in Florida, where the courts took a very conservative approach to child support.

As long as they were talking about money, she pressed forward. The rare opening gave her a chance to clarify things with a woman who'd seemed intent on getting her own way, without considering all the pluses and minuses.

"There's another possibility." Amanda paused. The more time she spent with Mitch, the more certain she was that he didn't deserve the hand he'd been dealt. Hailey averaged one meltdown per visit, yet Mitch never lost his patience or even spoke sharply to the child. If anything, Amanda was beginning to think he was too lenient with his headstrong daughter. "Let's assume Mitch somehow proves he didn't hurt Hailey."

At that, Karen's nostrils flared. Her head came up.

Amanda waved her hand. "I'm not taking a position here. That's up to the courts to decide. But, for the sake of argument, let's say he's able to prove that the accident occurred just the way he said it did."

Somewhat mollified, Karen nodded. "Okay," she said. "But just for the sake of argument."

"Eventually, Dobson could order joint custody. Then, based on Florida law, all expenses would be split right down the middle."

Karen's face turned pensive. "I guess that wouldn't be so bad. It's not like he's giving me a fortune right now."

Quickly, Amanda backtracked. "No. I mean *all* expenses. Day care. Tuition. Food. Right now Mitch pays for everything. You'd be responsible for half those costs, without the monthly stipend you're getting now."

"That's so not fair!" Karen stood and marched to the window overlooking the tiny patio. "Do you have any idea how difficult it is to work all day and come home to a child like Hailey? I'm telling you, she's a handful. There's never a break when she's around. It's not all fun and games."

Amanda rubbed her neck, where her veins pulsed with a rush of emotion. Karen was making progress, but she still had a lot to learn. Criticizing her wouldn't bring about a change in attitude. The situation called for a light touch.

"I know it's hard," she soothed. "Being a parent isn't just the occasional trips to Disney World. It's tough work being there for your daughter when she needs you. Reading her stories at night and tucking her in. Attending all those parent-teacher conferences and setting boundaries. It's a big price to pay for all the hugs and kisses, but it's a necessary one…for Hailey's sake."

Doubt filled Karen's eyes. "But for now I get, what—four hours off on the weekend? While Mitch is able to come and go as he pleases?"

"I think he'd trade places in under eight seconds."

The words tumbled from her lips before she had a

chance to think about them. Amanda held her breath, hoping she hadn't pushed too hard.

Karen's eyes narrowed. "That's the second time you've taken his side. You're not having second thoughts about representing me, are you?"

Amanda considered her answer carefully. Her opinion of Mitch *had* changed. She no longer saw him as the kind of man capable of physically harming his child. That didn't change her opinion of him as a father, however. Before Hailey's accident, the man had spent far too many nights working late at the office and far too few hours with his daughter. Karen, with her nine-to-five job at Bella's, was in a better position to offer Hailey the love and care she needed.

"No," she said at last. "I made a commitment and I'll see it through. If you want primary custody of Hailey, I'll do my best to get it for you." Just as she'd do her best to convince her client that every child deserved the love and attention of both parents.

Karen absorbed this new information with a nod. Her eyes watered when she sent a troubled look toward the sink filled with dirty dishes. "It's just so damn difficult. I want to do better. Honestly, I do."

"You're still adjusting to the situation, but I know what it's like to grow up around parents who don't have time for you. Trust me, you don't want to be that kind of person. For a long time, I thought I'd never have a family of my own because of the way my parents treated me. But now...well, maybe someday."

Hailey had sparked the first, tiniest urge to have a child of her own. The more time they spent together, the more Amanda thought she might be up to the challenge of motherhood. Of course, that meant there'd have to be a man in her life. Immediately, the image of a tall, dark-haired prosecutor flashed through her mind. She drummed her fingers on the table.

She'd grown closer to Mitch despite herself. She'd even begun to look forward to Sunday afternoons with him and Hailey. No, they hadn't crossed a line, but thoughts of him invaded her days and filled her nights even though she knew he was off-limits.

But what about after this case ends?

She shook her head, knowing this was the wrong time and place to dwell on her old boyfriend. She was a court-appointed lawyer assigned to supervise Mitch's visits with his daughter. And if that wasn't a good enough reason to keep her distance from the handsome attorney, she was also his ex-wife's lawyer. Amanda had a moral and legal obligation to do right by her client. So, no, there'd be no more thoughts of a future with Mitch Goodwin.

Across the table, Karen leaned forward.

"I'm glad you were straightforward with me about the child support. It makes what I asked you in here to discuss even more important." With a glance toward the hallway, Karen dropped her voice to a whisper. "I've heard rumors of expansion plans for Bella Designs." She frowned at the dowdy kitchen. "And since, from what you say, I can't expect Mitch to help me out, I've decided to apply for the manager's job at the new store."

Something in Karen's posture told Amanda there was bad news ahead. Almost unwilling to hear the answer, she asked, "Where?"

"Miami." The look in Karen's eyes hardened. "And as my lawyer, you can't tell a soul. Not even Mitch." She sat back in her chair. "Especially not Mitch."

Her promise to represent her client to the best of her abilities still rang in Amanda's ears. Though her stomach churned at the idea of keeping such a monumental secret from the man who thought the world revolved around his daughter, she had no choice. She ground her teeth together and nodded.

ON THE DECK behind the house, a cloud of meat-flavored smoke rose from the grill. It dissipated quickly in the moist summer air. Mitch grabbed a pair of tongs. After checking to see that the hot dogs were sufficiently charred—exactly the way Hailey liked them—he gently turned each one.

"Five minutes," he called to the young girls playing on the jungle gym he'd erected the Labor Day weekend Hailey turned two. "Time to get washed up."

He braced for an argument.

More often than not, getting preschoolers to come when they were called required the skills of a master cat herder. Today, with Amanda looking over his shoulder, it was doubly important that he fit the image of a perfect father. When their guests replied, "Yes, Mr. Goodwin," he relaxed and told himself there might be a benefit to Hailey spending time at her mom's, after all. Thanks to the weeks that had passed since his daughter and her friends had played together, all the girls were on their best behavior.

Mitch smiled, remembering how excited Hailey had been when Amanda's SUV had pulled to the curb. His daughter had literally jumped from the vehicle, her dark curls bouncing. She'd spent the first fifteen minutes racing around the house, checking to make sure that nothing had changed in her absence. Except for a bit more dust on the furniture and an overflowing laundry hamper in his bedroom, nothing had. When he'd announced that Emma and Reese were joining them, Hailey had been so happy, she'd danced around on her toes.

Closing the lid on the grill and firming his smile, Mitch wiped his hands down the front of the red apron Hailey had picked out for his birthday last year. He didn't fool himself. He owed this day to Amanda. He'd been darn lucky the day Dobson had appointed her to oversee Hailey's visits. No one else would have been so accommodating, letting them meet here at the house, even helping him get ready for the cookout. He crossed his fingers, hoping that seeing him in his element would sweep away her lingering doubts about the home he'd made for Hailey.

"All set over there?" He swung a glance in her direction and froze, held captive by an enticing rear view of denim shorts and a snug T-shirt that showed off tempting curves. A reaction that was anything but fatherly stirred within him.

"I think we're good." Amanda placed the last juice box beside a red plastic plate and smoothed a wrinkle from the checked tablecloth. She turned toward him, a few loose hairs spilling from the ponytail she'd hastily assembled after Mitch suggested they eat outside.

He resisted the urge to cross the deck and tuck the tendrils behind her ears. The last few weeks, he'd become familiar with her moods. Today, a slight stiffness in her shoulders hinted that something weighed heavily on her. Uncertain whether he was the source or not, he eyed her closely.

Was she having second thoughts about coming to his house? Were they breaking the rules by meeting here?

His gut told him that wasn't the problem. Ever since Hailey had coaxed Amanda into joining their tea party that first Sunday afternoon, the slim blonde had ignored the DCF rule book. Each Sunday, she joined in their games. Afterward, she and Hailey usually curled up on the couch, where Amanda read books to his daughter while he gathered up their toys and such at the end of the allotted visitation. Sure, she still made an effort to remain aloof and observant, but he could tell her heart wasn't in it.

Mitch ran a hand through his hair as he thought back to the Saddle Up Stampede and the way he'd held Amanda in his arms. He'd been amazed at his reaction then. She'd moved him in ways he hadn't experienced since the summer they'd spent at rodeo camp. Ever since, the slightest touch of her fingers on his arm had been intoxicating. A shared look from across the room could send his heart rate galloping.

He fought against a growing hunger for the woman who stirred his desire for white picket fences, two-point-five kids and laughter around the dinner table every night. He'd never been the kind of man who wanted a physical relationship without an emotional one, and he wondered if she fought the same churn of feelings.

"You doing okay?" he asked.

"Sure," she said without meeting his gaze. "Why wouldn't I be?"

"You seem a little quieter than usual."

Amanda waved aside his concern. "It's not something I can talk about right now."

The very fact that they couldn't discuss it meant whatever was bothering her had to do with him. Or more to the point, the custody case. Questions formed on his tongue. Before he could ask them, a trio of excited young girls trouped up the steps of the deck.

With his concerns about Amanda shoved to one side,

he swung his attention to the children. "What have we here, the princess and her court?"

He bowed deeply, his hand sweeping out to encompass all the girls. They promptly erupted in giggles. He spun his hand in circles in a manner depicted by a thousand courtesans in a thousand movies, and the children laughed harder. Their happiness warmed his heart, and the next hour sped by.

Shortly after Hailey's favorite meal of burned hot dogs, homemade mac 'n' cheese, and grapes disappeared, Lydia dropped by for Reese and Emma. Though Mitch expected the usual whines and wails when her friends left, Hailey only asked if she could play in her room. With Mrs. Giggles perched on her hip, she headed up the stairs. Minutes later, laughter and the sounds of a little girl talking to her dolls drifted into the kitchen.

"She had a good time today." At the sink, Amanda's voice rose above the sound of running water. "I was afraid she'd be upset after our talk this morning about the accident."

Mitch glanced at the ceiling. "Yeah," he said softly. "She seems okay with it. So." He hesitated. "She doesn't remember anything?"

"No. Afraid not." Amanda's ponytail swung back and forth. "Not the fall. Not going to the park. Nothing, until she woke up in the hospital the next day."

Mitch brushed aside a sharp jab of regret. Hailey's account of that evening had been his best hope for bringing his daughter home permanently. He ran a hand through his hair, doubt niggling at him.

Should he have trusted his ex-wife's lawyer to handle such an important conversation?

Did he trust Amanda?

He did, and though the truth of that surprised him,

it shouldn't have. After his visits with Hailey, they'd spent hours laughing about old times, reconnecting. He'd discovered the grown-up Amanda was far more intriguing than the young girl he'd once loved. He could count on her to tell him the truth. Even if a lie would better serve her client's interests.

"So, what did you think about our little cookout?" he asked, resisting the urge to press for details.

Water sluiced from the casserole dish Amanda had finished rinsing. "Is this how you and Hailey usually spend your weekends? Or were you doing things differently to impress me?" She tilted the pan upside down in the dish drainer before turning to face him.

Puzzled, Mitch let his gaze sweep past the kitchen to the deck where they'd eaten. While it was true he'd hoped Amanda would see his best side today, he hadn't gone to extraordinary lengths.

"I'm not sure I know what you mean. It was a typical Sunday afternoon. It's the one day of the week Hailey and I always spend together. If the weather's nice, like today, we cook out. If not, I make pasta." He grimaced as the wave of bad memories from the last time he'd fixed spaghetti rolled over him. "Or something. About half the time, a few of Hailey's friends will join us."

"My experience with families is somewhat limited." Amanda tipped her head as if to remind him that the admission counted as a world-class understatement. "But it seems like, even in restaurants, either the mom or the dad is always on a cell phone. Checking their email. Texting. You don't."

It was good that she'd noticed, Mitch told himself. There were other things he wanted Amanda to know about the way the Goodwin household operated.

"Any other day of the week, I'm as guilty of that as

the next guy. Monday through Saturday, Esme takes care of Hailey. I rarely see her much before bedtime. To be honest, when I'm working a trial, I may not even get a chance to read her a bedtime story or tuck her in at night." He hated that part, but he wasn't going to lie about it. "Saturdays are busy. Dance lessons. Soccer practice. Whatever. And birthday parties—you wouldn't believe how many of those there are."

At the mention of birthdays, his thoughts took an unexpected detour.

"Will you ask Karen if she's received any mail for Hailey?" He stared into the distance, hoping the neighborhood rumor mill had churned out Karen's address, fearing it hadn't.

"Sure." Amanda shrugged. "Are you looking for something in particular?"

"Those parties I mentioned. One or two invitations arrive in the mail every week, but I haven't gotten any since..." He let a simple gesture indicate the day his world had turned upside down. It was one thing to make him a social pariah. His daughter shouldn't have to suffer for it.

"I'll check." Amanda's fingers trailed across the granite countertop. "You live a much different life than I'd pictured."

Was that a hint of longing in her voice? "I hope that's a good thing," he said.

"Oh, it is."

Her sweet, wistful look was one of his favorite expressions, and his hunger for her stirred. Intending only to brush his mouth against hers, he leaned down, but he couldn't help himself. He had to taste her. He swept his tongue across her lips, savoring the hint of familiarity he found there.

Her lips parted. Whether she wanted a breath, or more of him, he didn't know and he didn't care. He swept in, his mouth possessing hers in a move that felt more right than anything else had in a long time. For a few minutes, there was no custody case, no injured daughter, no supervised visitation. His troubles faded so completely that there was only Amanda and the incredible feel of her lips against his.

They kissed until their tongues danced and his breath turned ragged. His heart thundered in his chest.

Wanting to follow the kiss wherever it might lead, Mitch shifted forward. He slid his hand around Amanda's waist, his fingers brushing the counter behind her. At a quiet thunk from upstairs, he froze.

In an instant, they had pulled apart.

Calling himself ten kinds of fool for letting things go so far, Mitch put a finger to his lips. "I'll be right back," he whispered.

Silently, he climbed the stairs, while doubts flooded in to fill the spaces where moments before there had been only Amanda and the kiss. Outside Hailey's room, he paused long enough to gather the remnants of his composure before he eased the door open and peered inside.

His daughter lay curled up on her bed, one thumb in her mouth. The sight brought a painful smile to his lips. How many Sunday afternoons had Hailey protested that she was too old for naps, only to drift off on the couch, or while playing in her room? After all the excitement she'd had, coming home and seeing her friends, he should have expected it.

He crossed to her bedside and picked Mrs. Giggles up from the floor. When he placed her next to Hailey, his daughter stirred, reaching out one arm to clutch the doll to her chest. Mitch brushed hair from Hailey's forehead and tried not to grimace. He had no business kissing Amanda while his daughter was in the same county, much less the same house.

Determined to keep a tighter leash on his libido, he was on his way downstairs to apologize when the phone rang. He snatched the receiver from the cradle in his office before the third ring. The muscles in his jaw jumped when he recognized Cheryl Johnson's voice on the other end of the line. They jumped again when he learned the woman's two nephews were waiting for him in her kitchen.

"I'll be right there," he said, unable to believe the chance to speak with Joey and Chuck had finally arrived.

He glanced through his office door to the kitchen, where Amanda stood. He needed to speak with her, to apologize for losing his head, to reassure her—and him—that their kiss wouldn't be repeated as long as the custody battle continued. But the opportunity to speak with the boys who could clear his name might not come again soon. He couldn't miss it.

Mitch squared his shoulders. He had to go, but no one said leaving was easy. He picked up his keys and crossed the living room to say goodbye.

THOUGH KISSING MITCH felt like coming home, there was nothing Norman Rockwell about the way she had melted in his arms or how their tongues had thrust and parried until her breath had been reduced to soft pants. Nothing warm and fuzzy about the way his strong hands had cupped her face or pulled her to him until his thighs pressed against hers.

No, kissing Mitch was all power and emotion. Stirring and wanting. His touch stole her breath and robbed her of coherent thought. And that was just…wrong.

She pressed her fingers to lips that still throbbed.

Where did they go from here?

She'd spent hours with Mitch and Hailey, enough time that she was convinced he would never harm his child. But it was a total conflict of interest for them to become physically involved. She was still his ex-wife's attorney and an officer of the court. As recently as a few hours ago, she'd reaffirmed her promise to help Karen gain full custody of Hailey. If that wasn't bad enough, the woman's latest secret spelled doom with a capitol *D* for the slightest hope of a future with Mitch. When the truth came out—and Amanda had no doubt it would—he'd never forgive her.

And even if kissing Mitch didn't break every rule in the book, she could never get involved with a man who chose his job over his family. Mitch did exactly that, spending only one day a week with his child.

No, she had no business kissing Mitch. Much less wanting to do it again.

The air conditioner kicked on, sending a blast of cold air into the space where Mitch had been standing only minutes before. Amanda caught her lip between her teeth. She leaned back against the counter, her ankles crossed, and tried to figure out how to tell the man she'd just kissed like a crazy woman that they could never— ever—do it again.

Mitch, apparently, had no such concerns. As she rubbed her arms against a sudden chill, he walked into the kitchen, his expression stern, his car keys clutched in his hand.

"Problems?" she asked. She scanned his face, noting a tremor of excitement that seeped around the edges of his frown.

"Nothing important."

Somehow, she doubted that. She gave him a closer look. The hair she'd mussed had been smoothed back into place.

"I need to dash out for a minute. I'll be right back. Would you mind staying with Hailey while I'm gone?"

"You're going out? Some kind of emergency?"

Mitch shrugged. "No, nothing like that. Ordinarily, I'd put it off, but since Hailey's asleep…"

A chip of the pedestal she'd erected in case Mitch turned out to be one of the good guys flaked onto the floor.

Amanda buried a sting of rejection behind the steady smile she'd developed during her rodeo days. "And this can't wait another half hour until I take Hailey home?"

"I'll be back to say goodbye."

To Hailey. But not to her.

"I can't promise I'll wait. Karen has plans for them this evening. I promised to have her back at six on the dot. Besides, you know the rules. Visitation must start and stop at the appointed times."

"So…" Mitch glowered. "We're back to the rules again?"

When she didn't respond, he wavered until she thought he might choose to stay. But his answer, when he finally reached a decision, was one she didn't expect.

"I have to go."

She knew then he had a secret and was hiding it from her. Had the district attorney called with some new case for him to handle? Had something come up in the office that couldn't wait till morning? Whatever it was, she'd bet her last dollar his work had once more interfered with his home life.

Precisely thirty minutes later, Amanda steeled herself and marched up the stairs. At the entrance to Hailey's room, her pique gave way to amazement. Pink floral wallpaper and soft carpeting turned the space into every little girl's fantasy, exactly the room Amanda had longed for when she was Hailey's age. Her glance took in the dollhouse on a low table, the shelves loaded with children's books, and more dolls than the average toy store. Beneath the wispy curtains of a bed canopy, she gently shook a tiny shoulder.

"Sweetheart," Amanda said in her softest voice. "Time to leave, honey."

The girl blinked sleepily and yawned. "Where's Daddy?"

"He had to go out for a bit. We'd wait for him, but your mommy is taking you to the movies, remember?" She sighed, glad that at least one Goodwin had learned the importance of spending time with their daughter.

Hailey sat up. Her feet dangled over the edge of the bed. "But I want to say bye."

The protest rekindled Amanda's anger at Mitch. He'd provided his child with all the trappings of a perfect life. Yet the man couldn't stick around long enough for a four-hour, court-appointed visitation. What kind of father did that make him, really?

"I'm sorry." Her heart went out to the child. "We need to leave now."

Hailey kept up a constant stream of objections as Amanda guided her down the stairs and to her car. With every step, the little girl's complaints rose in pitch, each a bit more frantic than the last, until Amanda feared Hailey was on the verge of one of her infamous meltdowns. Uncertain how she'd handle things if it came to that, she dredged her memory for some way to distract the child as she struggled to buckle Hailey into her car seat.

"Have I told you about the first time I performed in the rodeo?"

Hailey's feet drummed the leather upholstery. "I don't care." She threw herself against the seat back. "Stupid old rodeo. Stupid. Stupid. I wanna see my daddy."

Amanda took a calming breath and eased Hailey's arm under the seat belt. "I was just about your age. I got to wear a beautiful costume. It had sparkles."

Hailey's complaints stopped abruptly. She peered up, her expression owlish. "A lot of sparkles?"

"Hundreds." Amanda nodded. "Thousands." Certain she'd captured the little girl's attention, she closed the passenger door and climbed behind the wheel. "My saddle sparkled, too, and it was—" she paused long enough to let her voice fill with awe "—pink."

"You rode a horse? A real horse?"

"Mmm-hmm. She was the prettiest little filly you'd ever see. Her name was Biscuit. Can you guess what color she was?"

"Was she brown?"

"That's exactly right. She was a pale brown. Just like a biscuit."

While Hailey listened in openmouthed interest, Amanda filled the ride home with stories of her earliest days on the rodeo circuit. By the time they reached Karen's apartment complex, the little girl had apparently forgotten her missing dad. In fact, she was so enthralled that Amanda had to promise to tell her more about the rodeo the following Sunday.

On her way home, Amanda wished her own thoughts about Hailey's dad would fade as quickly as his daughter's. Unfortunately, ignoring her problems with the frustratingly attractive man wouldn't make them go away. She couldn't deny that he stirred her in ways no other man had ever done. Considering her attraction to him, it was no wonder she spent more time tossing and turning than actually sleeping at night.

But Mitch Goodwin, with his killer smile, his high pressure job and his azure-blue eyes, was exactly the kind of man she'd sworn to avoid. The type who could never put her first in his life. What happened today had only proved her point. She had to stay away from him.

Tears gathered in her eyes. She dashed them aside with a stern reminder that she'd reached a smart decision, the only right one. When that didn't help, she made a quick stop at a grocery store, where she filled a cart with chocolate and doughnuts and other heart-soothing essentials. Knowing it wouldn't drown her sorrows, she hesitated over a bottle of wine before deciding that marinating her troubles for a bit couldn't hurt.

The motor home parked beside her house erased all hope of indulging in a few hours of self-pity. Amanda studied the figure sitting in her favorite rocker by the front door. Looking immense in a plaster cast, his foot rested on the rail that ran along the porch.

Afraid her day had just gone from bad to worse, she lifted a questioning look to her father's face.

The man didn't waste time with pleasantries.

"Where the hell have you been, baby girl?" he demanded.

Chapter Eight

"Dad?" Amanda hurried up the walkway between rows of neatly trimmed hibiscus.

Paint flakes littered the porch beneath her father's ankle. From the looks of things, he'd been hanging out in front of her house for quite some time. She scanned the area, looking for beer or soda cans, a bottle of water. Seeing none, she glanced at the decorative thermometer on the wall behind him. The mercury had climbed past eighty-five.

"You must be dying in this heat."

"I've spent my whole life in arenas where the temperature never dropped below a hundred," Tom groused in typical fashion. "Guess I can handle a couple of hours in the shade."

Amanda ignored a guilty twinge and stifled the urge to feel sorry for him. How was she supposed to know her dad was in the state? He hadn't bothered to call. Not since the night of Hailey's accident. She lowered her purse and the bagful of groceries onto an empty chair.

"Well, I'm surprised to see you. How've you been?"

"Not so good, in case you hadn't noticed." He raised his foot an inch, pointing as if she were blind or oblivious. "I'm sittin' here with a busted leg, ain't I?"

"I see that, Dad."

She sucked her tongue between her teeth and bit down. Broken bones notwithstanding, he'd always been too busy for visits with his only child. Which meant he needed something.

"Hand me them crutches, will ya?"

She reached for the pair he'd propped against the house, bracing herself for one of her father's impossible demands. "What happened?"

"Some fool in Bonifay tossed a firecracker into the ring during the show. You know Brindle never was big on noises. He shied. I fell."

Amanda winced. "How's Brindle?"

"Mighta' known you'd be more concerned about the horse than me." Tom sank back in his chair. "Can't you see I'm the one sittin' here all busted up?"

Amanda took a deep breath and counted to five. This wasn't the first time her father had gotten hurt during a performance. Apart from the year she'd turned thirteen, when three broken ribs had cost him his last chance at a gold buckle, she could cite at least a dozen trips to emergency rooms in as many towns.

"I assumed that since you made it this far, you were okay. Is it just the leg? Nothing else? No concussion?" At his age, he was lucky he hadn't broken his neck.

"Ain't that enough, baby girl?"

"Enough to keep you from riding for a month or two. Is that why there's a motor home parked in my driveway?"

Tom ignored her question in favor of one of his own. "Where've you been, anyway? I've been sittin' here waiting for you all afternoon." He eased his leg from the rail with a groan and grunted his way onto the crutches.

"Guilty as charged." She hoped the quip would distract him from the heat that crept up her neck and onto her face. Part of the time her dad had been sweltering on the porch, she'd been in Mitch's arms. A mistake, sure, but she couldn't afford to give her old man ammunition to use against her.

She needn't have worried. Her father never even glanced her way.

"I wish we had time to sit and talk, gal, but you'd best be gettin' to packin'. You'll need to be hittin' the road early if you're gonna make Austin by the weekend."

Amanda blinked slowly, trying to push back the sense of disaster that had threatened ever since she'd spotted her dad's vehicle in the drive. Her voice chilled. "What makes you think I'm going anywhere?"

Tom drew himself as erect as he could, considering the crutch propped under each arm. "I heard you did real good at the Saddle Up. I'm right proud of you."

Flattery was not going to get him anywhere. While she'd like to think her dad had reached out to her in a time of crisis, she knew better. He'd landed on her doorstep only because he thought he could use her in some way.

She stared, waiting him out, certain she was right.

Tom met her unflinching gaze with one of his own. "You gonna make me beg?" Annoyance laced his slow drawl. "You know I've got a full slate of appearances scheduled. I need you to fill in for me till my leg's healed up. You already know the routine. Besides, you're family."

Amanda's back went ramrod stiff. There'd been a time when she'd have done practically anything to earn her father's respect, his love. The barn door had slammed shut on those days.

Too bad he hadn't gotten the memo.

Movement on the sidewalk caught her attention. She

waved to a neighbor, Mrs. Carrington, and her dog, Ginger. Airing the sad tale of the Markette family history while the entire block listened in was not on Amanda's agenda. She retrieved her purse and the bag of groceries, unlocked the front door and held it wide.

"You want a glass of iced tea, Dad? Come on in and I'll fix you some. You can drink it while you handle those calls you'll need to make."

Awkwardly maneuvering on one leg and the crutches, Tom thumped across the porch. "What calls are you talking about?"

"The people you'll contact in order to find a replacement who isn't me," she said, when the door was safely closed behind him. "I have a life. A job I love. A place in this community. I'm not giving those things up. Not even for you."

Hot on her heels, Tom trifooted it across her living room and into the kitchen, where he slumped into a chair. Her gaze swung to his cast. Surely he hadn't made the long drive from north Florida with his broken leg propped up on the dashboard.

"How'd you get here, anyway?"

Tom shrugged. "Royce and Mavis. They were on their way down to Fort Lauderdale. They're taking a breather from the circuit and gonna stay with her family for a bit."

Amanda squinted. A "breather" was just another way of saying out of work.

"If I were you, I'd start with them." The answer seemed so obvious, she wondered why her father hadn't come up with it himself. She held out one hand, palm up. "Royce doesn't have any gigs." She added the second hand. "You have slots to fill. And Royce has been angling for a spot on the Markette team for as long as you've known him." She clapped her hands together. "Sounds like the perfect solution."

Angry sparks glinted in Tom's eyes. "You're serious? You ain't gonna help me? I've never asked you for nothing, and this is the way you treat me?"

At his scathing disbelief, Amanda's old hurts flared. Tom Markette had never had the time or inclination for anyone but himself. She thought of the summer after her mom had died. She'd begged to stay with him. Instead, he'd dumped her in a rodeo camp run by one of his pals and told her to make the most of her summer job as a camp counselor. Things hadn't improved as she'd gotten older. He hadn't even shown up the night she'd won a gold buckle in Las Vegas. Standing there, staring out into the crowds and knowing he wasn't among the thousands of cheering, clapping fans, she'd decided, once and for all, that she was done with trying to win his love.

She inhaled and let the breath seep out between her lips. This wasn't about revenge. It was about doing right for herself. She downed a long, steadying swallow from her own glass of tea.

"Better get in touch with Royce."

Her father sat, arms crossed, anger rolling from him in waves. Eyeing him, she realized she couldn't let him stay with her. Once he brought more than a toothbrush and a change of clothes into her house, she'd never have another moment's peace.

"I don't have a guest room, so you'll have to make do on the couch tonight. Tomorrow I'll start looking for a trailer park with hookups, so you'll have water and electricity."

There were several not too far away. Though she'd never forgive him, she couldn't abandon him completely. She'd shop for him, drop off groceries and supplies, whatever he needed, as long as he didn't try to ruin her life.

"I should have known it'd be like this," Tom sputtered. "You're a hardhearted, ungrateful girl, Mandy Markette. You know that?"

"Amanda," she corrected. "My name is Amanda. And if you want my help, you'd better remember it."

Tom shoved the chair next to him. His crutches clattered to the floor.

"What am I supposed to do about the horses? I can't exactly care for them while I'm laid up. Or did you stop to think about them?"

There hadn't been a horse trailer in her driveway. She looked through the window where a motor home blocked her view of the house next door.

"Where are Brindle and Daisy?"

"They're out at Boots and Spurs. I paid for them to stay overnight, since you don't have a backyard to speak of."

The way her father pronounced judgment on her half-acre of smoothly mowed grass elicited a chuckle, but her laughter faded as she considered her neighbors. What would they say if they spied two horses in her backyard? No matter. She'd enjoyed her weekend mornings at Boots and Spurs. Taking care of Brindle and Daisy would fit right into her plans to do more riding. And who knew? Maybe Hailey Goodwin would enjoy spending a Sunday afternoon at the stables. The little girl had certainly brightened at the mention of spangles and horses.

But when thinking of Hailey led to thoughts of Mitch, Amanda spun away, using the need to prepare a bed for her dad as an excuse to leave the room. As she went about gathering sheets and linens for a one-night stay, she had to admit that Mitch, unlike her own father, made the most of the little time he did spend with his daughter.

Minutes later, she shook out the top sheet, letting it billow before it settled down over the cushions on the couch. Back in the day, when she'd been performing with her dad or going for the next win on the rodeo circuit, she'd learned that timing was everything. A tenth of a second here, another one there, and the entire routine could fall apart. Though Amanda had sworn to avoid Mitch and his mind-boggling kisses from now on, Karen's plans to relocate complicated the tense situation between them. Already on edge, Amanda felt sure her dad couldn't have picked a worse time to show up on her doorstep.

MITCH SETTLED THE CARDBOARD TRAY holding his coffee and the soda Amanda preferred on the stoop outside her office. His stomach grumbled at the smells of yeast and chocolate, apple and a hint of spice that wafted from the bulging bag he wedged between their drinks. Though he'd asked the woman behind the counter of the doughnut shop for one of everything, he refused to help himself to so much as a nibble. The young girl he'd once loved had devoured sticky, sweet cinnamon buns like there was no tomorrow, but he had no idea what she ate for breakfast these days. The last thing he wanted was to pull a doughnut from the bag, only to discover he'd eaten Amanda's favorite. That certainly wouldn't bode well for the thanks he owed her for watching Hailey last night.

He surveyed the immediate area, checking to make sure an army of ants hadn't caught the scent and lined up on the sidewalk, prepared to march in his direction. Not a single six-legged creature crawled within biting distance. Loosening his tie, he brushed off a place for himself.

A different kind of hunger stirred when, at a few minutes before nine, Amanda stepped from her SUV and made her way to the stairs. The day's light breeze fluttered the neckline of her camisole, showing a hint of perfect cleavage beneath an unbuttoned jacket. A suit skirt clung so tightly to her shapely legs that the fabric outlined her trim thighs with every step. One glimpse of the open-toed shoes cupping her slim feet and he swallowed, envisioning what might follow if he gave her a foot massage.

A trickle of sweat threatened to escape his hairline. He wiped it away, not giving it a chance to run down his cheek before he waved a greeting. His eyes narrowed at the tight-lipped scowl Amanda sent him in return.

Not the welcome expression he'd been expecting. Straightening his shoulders, he stared at the loose curls that had escaped a smooth updo to soften the harsh lines of Amanda's frown. His mouth went dry. So much depended on her cooperation, if not her actual help. Yet all he wanted was to take her into his arms and kiss her senseless. He pushed aside his own desires with a reminder that he was here for Hailey. And when Amanda neared, he found his voice.

"I come in peace," he said. Liquid sloshed as he lifted the tray.

"Busy night?" Amanda's pace didn't slow. She brushed past him, briskly inserting keys in locks and shutting off alarms. Before she could slam the door in his face, he followed her inside.

"You said you'd be back before I had to take Hai-

ley home." The snaps on Amanda's briefcase opened
with a volley of tiny explosions. "Hailey wasn't very
happy with you."

She wasn't the only one.

He could see that now, and wished he'd handled
things differently. But, like everything else in his relationship with Amanda, last night had been complicated. Walking back into the house after speaking with
Cheryl's nephews, Mitch had been eager to share his
news with the one person who would understand its
importance. A sinkhole had opened in his chest when
he'd realized she was gone.

When he thought about it, that was the minute he'd
known how much she meant to him. He'd counted on
her to be there. He looked forward to their time together
on Sunday afternoons almost as much as he did the time
he spent with Hailey. This morning, he hadn't been able
to stand the thought of waiting a week to see Amanda
again. His good news gave him the perfect excuse.

If she'd even speak to him…

The way she stared at him, he had his doubts.

"I'm sorry," Mitch said simply. "I hope you'll understand once I explain."

"What? That your work is more important than Hailey?" She waited a beat. "Or me?"

She was wrong if she thought he'd willingly walk out
on his daughter for something so mundane as his job.
Now was his chance to prove it. He took a deep breath
and forged ahead.

"The phone call was from a neighbor. It was about
the witnesses to Hailey's fall."

Amanda lost interest in the papers she'd been shifting from her briefcase to her desk. Hope and worry

poured into the glance she focused on him. "Not your office? Not the district attorney?"

Knowing he should have anticipated her reaction, Mitch mentally gave himself a swift kick in the pants. How many hot summer nights had he held Amanda in his arms while she cried because, once again, her father had chosen his career over her? Too many to count, for sure. His own parents had planned a family vacation around the end of summer camp, staying for the mini rodeo and closing ceremonies even though he was a counselor and one of the oldest in attendance. Not Amanda's dad. He hadn't even cared enough to show up. Instead, he'd sent her a bus ticket.

Mitch cringed, thinking how badly that must have hurt her. But he wasn't like her father. He hurried to correct the misconception.

"The boys—young men, actually—they're older than I remembered. They're from Tampa. The day Hailey got hurt, they'd been visiting a neighbor, their aunt Cheryl. I've tried everything short of issuing a subpoena to get in touch with them."

Encouraged when curiosity gradually replaced the last vestiges of anger on Amanda's face, he pushed on. "She called to let me know the boys had dropped by on their way home from the beach. I couldn't risk missing them again."

"Did you speak with them?" Amanda asked hesitantly.

Mitch nodded. "Joey, the youngest, had his back turned. He didn't see a thing. The other one, Chuck, actually saw Hailey fall from the monkey bars. He's willing to testify to that in court."

"Oh." Amanda's hand fluttered against her chest,

her standard reaction whenever life took an unexpected turn. "That's good news," she breathed.

"It is, isn't it?" A fresh wave of the relief he'd felt while talking to the young men washed over him. Mitch studied Amanda, expecting to see her eyes mirror his excitement. His concern edged up a notch when she stared out the window of her office while something that looked an awful lot like worry creased her brow.

In case he hadn't been clear enough, he tried again. "With their sworn statements, I can finally prove Hailey's fall was exactly what I said it was—an accident. I can get my daughter back. And then…"

He swallowed. This was the hard part. He was putting his heart on the line, trusting their kiss yesterday meant as much to her as it did to him. He crossed the room to take Amanda's hands in his.

"Then, maybe you and I can look forward to more than a stolen kiss on a Sunday afternoon."

He refused to react when Amanda shook her head. The frown he didn't like seeing on her face had returned, along with the impression that she was hiding something. He stared into her green eyes, where storm clouds gathered, and braced himself for a lightning strike.

She pulled her hands from his grasp. "I'm glad for you, Mitch, but I think you're getting ahead of yourself."

Cool, calm and collected. That's the image he presented to a jury. No matter what happened in court, he never let the twelve men and women in the box see him sweat. He was the man with the plan. Secure in the knowledge that if something went wrong, even his contingencies had contingencies.

Now he froze, while his thoughts raced. Had he misread her? Granted, they hadn't actually discussed the future, but based on their growing connection these past weekends, he'd hoped that once this case was behind them, they could build on the relationship they'd started that summer so long ago.

Didn't she want the same thing?

Amanda's fingers trailed along his forearm, stirring a faint hope, which faded when her hand dropped to her side.

"Even with this new evidence, Dobson won't order a change in custody before November," she pointed out. "Until then, Karen's my client. You're still on the opposite side of the aisle. We're already walking a legal tightrope. I don't think we can talk about the future until this is all resolved. Do you?"

Mitch ran a hand over his damp brow. She was right, of course. He'd been so excited at the prospect of bringing his daughter home that he'd lost sight of the big picture. Still, Amanda hadn't said no. Several hurdles stood between where they were and the day they could move forward with their lives. But as long as they had the same direction in mind, he could live with things the way they were…for now.

"Until then, I guess we'll have to settle for friendship. That okay with you?"

A faint smile creased Amanda's face. "Friends it is."

"In that case, I've brought you a gift."

"What is it?"

He grabbed the bag of doughnuts and held it open. The smell of yeast and sugar soon filled the air.

"Good friends?" he suggested, waving the bag in front of her nose.

Amanda's gaze dropped to the doughnuts. "The best," she agreed. She smiled and reached for the sack. "Ohhhh…"

He waited until she found a jelly-filled covered in powdered sugar before he snagged a glazed doughnut for himself. Moments later, he tried not to stare at the circle of white that dusted Amanda's lips, but the view was simply too tantalizing. He reached forward to brush the sugar from her mouth, but froze with his thumb pressed against her lower lip, staring. Sounds from the outer offices signaled the arrival of her receptionist and other staff, snapping him out of his daze. As they stepped apart, he peered into Amanda's upturned features and decided he'd never tire of the view. A drive to put that same slightly dreamy expression on her face every day for the rest of his life stirred, and he let his hand rest on her shoulder. But honoring her request, he shoved down the urge to confess his feelings and forced himself to talk about something else.

"Now that I have proof about what happened the night Hailey got hurt, I'm going to ask Judge Dobson for an early hearing," he whispered.

Amanda stiffened beneath his fingers. She shifted away from his touch.

"Don't tell me that," she said firmly. "When it comes to your custody case, I am not your friend. I'm opposing counsel. You wouldn't reveal your strategy in trial to a defense attorney, would you?"

He shook his head, and she continued. "In this case, there are rules that we have to follow. You can't tell me anything about your plans, and I can't talk to you about mine. It'll take some effort, but if there's any hope of getting through this, that's the way it has to be."

The sensation that she was hiding something moved within him again. He brushed a hand through his hair, pushing the feeling aside. His case to retain custody of his daughter was so much stronger than her absentee mother's that any plan to take Hailey away from him was bound to fail. He had no secrets, no skeletons in his closet. Hailey's accident was the only ammunition his ex-wife could have possibly used against him. Now that he had a witness to the fall, even that wouldn't be enough to sway Judge Dobson to Karen's side.

Knowing he had nothing to lose, and wanting to ease Amanda's worries, he quickly agreed to follow her rules. A few minutes later, he whistled as he headed to his car. Amanda had chosen the losing side in the custody battle for his daughter. Yet he couldn't fault her for doing her job. Beneath her soft exterior beat the heart of a woman who knew what she wanted and wasn't afraid to go after it.

To be honest, her drive was one of the things he liked best about her.

Yes, Amanda Markette was a woman of many facets. And he looked forward to discovering every one of them.

HAILEY TUGGED ON MITCH'S arm, urging him forward. When he didn't move fast enough across the straw-covered floor to suit his fleet-footed daughter, she slipped her arm out of her sling and tugged with both hands.

"Hailey," Mitch warned. "Your shoulder."

He motioned for Amanda to keep going while he stopped long enough to anchor Hailey's tiny elbow in the blue cloth.

"Stupid old sling," she muttered.

He leaned down to whisper in her ear. "Watch your language."

At last week's parent-teacher conference, he and Karen had been surprisingly civil to one another while Mrs. Birch commented on their daughter's expanding vocabulary…and not in a good way. The woman hadn't come right out and said so, but they'd received her message loud and clear. The turmoil in Hailey's life was having a negative effect. Though Mitch was certain his child would settle down once they put the custody case behind them, he was forced to correct her. "We don't say 'stupid.'"

His four-year-old's adorable face scrunched and she peered up at him. "But, Daddy, I can't use my fingers."

"You must wear the sling. You cannot say bad words."

He held on tight when she tried to pull away, while a series of nickers sounded through the big, drafty barn. Halfway down the long row of stalls, Amanda stopped in front of one. She lifted a latch, swinging open the top half of a wide Dutch door. An immense brown head poked into the aisle.

Hailey turned into a statue, her cute little mouth forming a perfect oval. She peered up at Mitch with wide blue eyes. "Can I pet him?"

Unease shifted beneath Mitch's ribs. Bringing his preschooler to Boots and Spurs suddenly didn't feel quite as smart as it had originally. Amanda had assured him that Daisy was the sweetest horse he'd ever meet, and he'd been fine with that…until he caught his first glimpse of the mare. At fourteen hands, Daisy might have the world's greatest disposition, but she still towered over his little girl.

"Can I, Daddy?" Hailey's imploring glance squeezed his heart.

He sought reassurance in Amanda's eyes. Her quiet confidence hushed his fears. With the realization of how much he trusted the green-eyed beauty, a smile sprang to his lips. He'd already placed his heart in her safekeeping. Surely, between the two of them, they could protect his little girl.

He turned to Hailey. "You have to listen to Miss Amanda and do everything just the ways she tells you. Okay?"

Delight sparkled in his daughter's eyes and she bobbed her head. With his permission, she ran down the aisle between the stalls to Amanda's side.

Assured that his daughter was in good hands, Mitch decided he could afford a moment to study Amanda in her element. Above scuffed and gouged boots, her snug jeans hugged every curve, stirring Mitch's desire to find the nearest bed of straw and put it to good use. With a quick reminder that they'd decided on infinitely smaller steps, and that his daughter was present, he shifted his focus higher. Light glinted off sequins surrounding the image of a bucking bronco on the T-shirt Amanda had worn for Hailey's sake. Beneath a tired old cowboy hat, her hair trailed down her back in a single long plait.

"Hey, tenderfoot," called the woman of his dreams. "You coming?"

"Yeah. Yeah, sure." He stopped woolgathering and put his feet in motion.

By the time he reached them, she had helped Hailey onto a step stool placed in front of the stall door. Mitch bit back a last-minute reservation when Amanda took his daughter's good hand in hers and demonstrated the right way to stroke the horse's cheek.

"He's prickly!" Hailey squealed.

Half expecting the mare to shy, Mitch almost snatched his child from the stool and out of harm's way. His trust in Amanda steadied him. A trust that was rewarded seconds later when Daisy only leaned closer.

"You want to use your inside voice when you're in

the barn with the horses," Amanda coached. "And Daisy's a girl. She might not like it if you keep calling her a boy."

Hailey nodded wordlessly. Her first tentative touches quickly gave way to gentle pats. Soon, she was stroking the long neck and jaw as though she'd been around horses all her life.

Mitch, accustomed to dealing in nanoseconds whenever his daughter was around, thought they'd established a new world's record when Hailey remained focused for nearly thirty minutes. When the little girl's attention began to wane, he didn't need to prompt Amanda, however. She was ready with the next task and moved them to it quickly.

"Daisy's used to getting treats whenever I come to see her. Can you guess her favorite?"

Mitch chuckled at Hailey's hopeful "Chocolate?"

"Nope." A warm smile broke across Amanda's face. "Carrots. You want to give her some?" She pulled one from the bag she carried. "Daisy's quite the little lady. She doesn't bite. Some horses do, though. You never want to feed a horse you don't know."

Hailey watched Amanda's every move as she demonstrated the best way to lay the carrot in the flat of her palm. Almost before Mitch considered objecting, the petite blonde held his daughter up so Daisy could gently lip the vegetable from her outstretched hand.

"Her mouth tickles." Hailey giggled.

Daisy's table manners were somewhat lacking. She crunched her treat loudly, her powerful jaws flexing with every bite.

Hailey looked over her shoulder at him. "Her teeth are really big."

Instead of being scared, she reached into the bag

and drew out another carrot. All by herself this time, she fed it to the horse, following every step Amanda had shown her.

"Can I ride her, Daddy?" Hailey asked moments after the last carrot disappeared down Daisy's throat.

Mitch gulped. The thought of his little girl on the back of the big mare was enough to make him lose sleep at night. Relieved that Hailey's shoulder provided an excuse, he answered, "Not today, honey. Your doctor says your arm isn't all better yet. Another couple of weeks."

He smiled, knowing that Hailey's shoulder was fully healed. She rarely used the sling anymore, resorting to it only when she was extremely tired or didn't get her own way.

"Then can I ride her, Daddy?"

So much for his hope that she'd lose interest. A quick glance at Amanda gave him the encouragement he needed. "Sure, honey," he said, making a vague promise. "But right now, Miss Amanda has some other things to show you."

To Hailey's delighted squeals, Amanda introduced his daughter to a surprise waiting in the next stall. Horses were one thing, but long-eared rabbits were soft and furry and had the added benefit of filling a little girl's lap. Hailey immediately plopped down near the cage door and began what promised to be a lengthy session of petting and babying the hand-raised bunnies.

Amanda propped her elbows beside his on the low stall's top rail.

"Did I tell you my dad's in town?" she asked quietly.

"Oh?" Mitch aimed a puzzled look in her direction. They'd talked on the phone this week, but she hadn't said a word about her father. Was that her big secret?

Glad that they finally had it out in the open, he asked, "And how's that going?"

"Well, he's as crotchety as ever." She gave a nervous laugh. "He busted his leg up in Bonifay, and of course expected me to hit the road, perform in the gigs he'd lined up. I set him straight on that score."

The thought of Amanda leaving shook him more than Mitch liked to admit. He breathed a silent prayer of thanks that she'd chosen to stick around, though the image of a father-daughter reunion didn't jibe with the emotionally wounded Amanda he'd once known. An old wariness crept over him. When they were teens, Tom Markette had made his way into practically every conversation, and Mitch had learned to tread carefully, never knowing when something he said would trigger an emotional blowup. He stretched, repositioning his arm so it touched Amanda's.

"How long's he staying?"

"Who knows? I thought it would only be a day or two, but he's asked if he can stay till his leg heals. By the way, I think I owe you one."

Mitch glanced at her. "How so?"

"Growing up, I always thought it was my fault he never wanted me around. Before my mom died, riding was the only way I could get his attention. After the car accident, things got worse between us. He stuck to himself, didn't want anything to do with me."

Mitch slipped one arm around Amanda's waist, offering her silent support while he listened.

"That summer at rodeo camp, you were always telling me I needed to think for myself, not see life through his eyes. I didn't—couldn't—listen back then."

She stopped for a breath while Mitch nodded. The freshness of her mother's death had only added to her confusion, and his whispered reassurances hadn't ever seemed to penetrate her layers of self-doubt. Feeling as if he had to say something, he told her the same thing he had back then. "You know the way your father behaved was never about you."

"I do now. I think I'm finally past all that. This visit has let me see him for who he really is—a self-centered, thoughtless man. You were right, all those times you told me it was never about me. He just doesn't care about anyone but himself. He's only here now because he doesn't have anywhere else to go."

She paused again. "You'd think I'd be hurt, but it's actually kind of freeing."

"Are you going to let him stay?" Mitch asked.

"I don't think that's a good idea. I've started looking for another place for him."

Self-confidence radiated from the woman who stood beside him, and Mitch's chest swelled with happiness for her. Though no one ever completely overcame the early loss of a parent, she'd found ways to cope. And now, apparently, she was dealing with the lingering issues with her father.

When Mitch stopped to think about it, the woman who stirred his heartstrings had grown into the kind of woman he wanted Hailey to become. And despite their decision to avoid a romantic relationship until the custody case was settled, Amanda played a huge role in the life he imagined.

Chapter Nine

Walking down the barn's center aisle, Amanda waved to
the stable hand she'd hired to exercise Brindle and Daisy
on the days she couldn't make it out to the dude ranch.
Days that came a lot more often than she'd planned in
the two weeks since her dad had made himself at home
on her couch. She tugged on the ends of the ponytail
she'd stuffed through the back of her baseball cap. This
morning, like most lately, she hadn't even had time to
braid her hair.

"You're frowning," Mitch said to Amanda when the
little girl at his side stopped talking long enough to
catch her breath. "Everything okay?"

She flexed her shoulders, where the weight of Kar-
en's secret pressed down. How honest could she be with
Mitch? She certainly couldn't tell him that his ex-wife
planned to move to Miami. If she broke client confi-
dentiality, she'd lose her license to practice law, pure
and simple. If she didn't, she risked any hope of a future with Mitch.

Not that they could even contemplate a future until
Hailey's custody was settled. So Amanda couldn't confess that she'd looked up from a case file yesterday and
realized she'd spent the past fifteen minutes daydream-
ing about him. Or that the way Hailey's arms twined

about her neck when she read stories to his little girl made her long for children of her own.

No, there was a lot she couldn't tell Mitch Goodwin. And without any easy solutions in sight, she stuck with what had become her standard answer. She focused on her dad and the trouble he'd brought into her life. Thanks to him and his constant demands, she'd been late getting to the office every day this week.

The weekend had been just more of the same.

"We pulled his mobile home around back. The neighbors aren't happy about it, but they're willing to look the other way. For now."

"No luck with the trailer parks?" Mitch asked.

"The snowbirds arrived early this year." An October freeze had moved through the Northeast, prompting many of Florida's winter residents to get a jump on the season. Prices had risen accordingly. "He's broke, and I'm having trouble finding an affordable spot."

"It's only for another month. That's something to be thankful for, right?"

She wished.

"More like three. His leg isn't mending the way it should. He might need surgery." She shrugged, determined to find a more cheerful subject. "Enough about him..."

She switched her focus to the little girl who skipped along, holding Mitch's hand. "Are you excited, Hailey?"

Questions and endless chatter had filled Amanda's car from the moment she'd strapped the child into her car seat until they arrived at the ranch. When Hailey had seen Mitch waiting for them, holding a shiny new riding helmet in little-girl pink, not even her seat belt could keep her from bouncing up and down. She'd flown from the vehicle the moment Amanda braked to a stop, and insisted on wearing the headgear immediately.

"Can Daisy go really fast? Can she jump over the fence?"

Amanda sent an amused glance toward Mitch. His lips had suddenly thinned. She couldn't blame him for having second thoughts. There was always an element of risk in putting a little kid on a horse, even one as gentle as Daisy. But there'd be no solo rides for Hailey. No jumping, either. Not for a long time.

Amanda eyed the active four-year-old. A very long time, she corrected. She reached for the child's hand. "Do you remember everything I taught you?"

They'd spent the last two Sundays getting ready for the big event.

Hailey stuck a finger between her chin and the strap on her helmet. "Daisy's my friend. I brush her. I give her carrots." She beamed at her newfound knowledge. "I'm going to ride today, aren't I?"

Amanda nodded and squeezed the little girl's shoulder.

They reviewed the tack next, Amanda accepting "syrup" for stirrup and "bite" for bit. Reins were not "giddy-ups," however, and she corrected the child while Hailey gave her helmet strap another tug.

"Too tight, Daddy. It squooshes me."

Mitch patted the hard, plastic top. "If you're going to ride, you have to wear it."

Amanda held her breath, waiting to see if Hailey would balk, hoping she wouldn't. The riding helmet was nonnegotiable. The child couldn't even enter the practice ring unless she agreed to wear it. When Hailey dropped her hand from the strap, Amanda put some extra wattage into her smile.

"And what rule do you always follow?"

"Always walk in front." The girl looked up importantly. "Horses can't see in back. They get scared."

"You're doing good, Hailey. What else?" Amanda sent Mitch a quick, reassuring glance. When startled, most horses kicked, protecting themselves the only way they could. But she and Mitch would watch Hailey like hawks, making sure the little girl stayed far away from flying hooves.

"Gentle, gentle." She softly patted an imaginary horse.

Despite the lessons, Amanda didn't take any chances. Once they arrived at Daisy's stall, she helped Hailey onto the step stool, holding tight to her shirt in case the horse made a sudden move. She watched closely while Hailey's hand got lost in the brush made for an adult's larger one.

"Great job, sweetheart." Under Mitch's constant encouragement, Hailey stuck with the task of giving Daisy a kid-size grooming. "You get a gold star."

And an A for effort, if not for skill, Amanda silently added. She smoothed Daisy's rumpled mane while the child hung the brush on a nearby hook. A few minutes later, after cinching Daisy's saddle tight, Amanda and the docile mount followed Hailey and her dad into the riding pen.

Mitch checked the strap on Hailey's helmet for what seemed like the tenth time before he settled his daughter in the saddle. With Amanda at the lead, and her dad never straying more than a foot from her side, Hailey held the reins just the way she'd been shown. They walked in circles, staying close to the rail. Hailey kept up a constant flow of chatter.

"You're a good horse, Daisy. Isn't she a good horse,

Daddy? I like riding. Can you see me, Daddy? Are you watching, Miss Amanda? Do you see me?"

But after three trips around the ring, Hailey grew bored with all the attention. She pushed at Mitch's arm around her waist.

"Let me do it, Daddy."

Amanda caught his questioning glance and sent Mitch a warning look. He might be Hailey's father and a good horseman in his own right, but she was doubly responsible for the child's safety—both for having arranged this riding lesson, and for being the court-appointed guardian whenever Hailey visited her dad. Amanda stepped into the bad cop role.

"Not today, sweetheart."

"I can. I can do it myself. Let go." Hailey slapped the reins and rocked in the saddle, urging the horse forward.

Amanda tugged on the bridle strap. The move pulled Daisy's head down and back. At the signal to stop, her immense hooves sank into the sand and her tail swished. She heaved a lip-fluttering breath of air.

Insistent, Hailey flapped the reins again. "Let go, Daddy." Her voice rose to a feverish squeal.

Amanda patted the velvet nose, reassuring Daisy that everything was under control. But when the horse's ears gave the barest twitch, she pinned Hailey with her best no-nonsense stare. "You need a lot of practice before you sit on a horse all by yourself."

"But I want to go fast!"

It was one thing for Hailey to raise her voice. It was quite another for her to break the rules. When her feet pummeled Daisy's sides, Amanda swept the startled child from the saddle and placed her firmly on the ground. Her resolute tone cut through the four-year-old's litany of complaints.

"Hailey, we talked about this. I said no kicking and I meant it. That's it for today. No more riding."

Hailey tilted her face up, her expression turning saucy. Her little hands fisted at her waist.

"No. You are not the boss of me," she taunted.

Amanda stood her ground when the child kicked, sending up a shower of dirt.

"Daddy will get me my own horse. A fast one."

Seeing Hailey strike the demanding pose and hearing her issue the ridiculous statement would have been comical if Mitch had done anything other than kneel beside his daughter and embrace her. Daisy's reins tight in her grasp, Amanda folded her arms across her chest. She wasted a who-does-she-think-she's-kidding look on Mitch.

"You might try telling her no, once in a while. It's not a four-letter word, you know."

Amanda almost clamped a hand over her mouth, unable to believe she'd said the words she'd been thinking out loud. Who was she to tell Mitch how to raise his daughter? She wasn't Hailey's mom. She wasn't anyone's mom. She might be dangerously close to giving her heart to the man who clutched his angry toddler so protectively, but they'd deliberately steered clear of discussing their future. Or her role in Hailey's upbringing.

Not that, if Karen moved them to Miami, Amanda could have any chance of ever finding out what her role might be.

Hands outstretched, she backed away. "Sorry," she mumbled. "I shouldn't have said anything. I'm sorry."

For a moment, the usual sounds of the ranch faded. Somewhere in the background, leather creaked and metal jangled as the mare shook her head. Instinctively, Amanda slid her hand along the horse's neck to grasp the bridle. She patted Daisy's nose again, this time only vaguely aware of the soft blowing kisses, the brush of a silken mane while she waited for a rightfully angry Mitch to tell her she'd overstepped her bounds.

A ripple spread across the big man's shoulders. Amanda's focus narrowed as a second shiver followed the first, and then a third, before understanding broke through her fear that she'd said too much. Over Hailey's shoulder, Mitch looked up at her, his face wreathed in smiles.

Warmth and the glint of an emotion she'd never expected to see sparkled in his azure eyes. Her heart thudded as, suddenly, the idea of a future with Mitch didn't seem as far-fetched as it once had. She pondered this new possibility while Mitch got to his feet.

One of his arms encircled her shoulders, the other resting on Hailey's helmet. His contagious laughter enveloped Amanda. Even Hailey quickly forgot her pique and joined in.

The first to laugh, Mitch was also the first to recover. When his laughter died to the occasional hiccup, he wiped his eyes. He captured his little girl's attention in a laserlike gaze.

"Hailey, I love you more than you will ever know, but I will not buy you a horse."

Amanda saw Mitch struggle to suppress a fresh wave of chuckles, and knew if she continued to watch she'd erupt in giggles, too. She clamped a hand over her mouth and ducked her head.

"It was wrong for you to kick Daisy," Mitch continued. "You need to apologize to her. And to Miss Amanda."

In Mitch's arms, a contrite Hailey petted Daisy's wide neck, whispering how sorry she was. Whether the mare realized what all the fuss was about or not, Amanda didn't know. But the sweetness of Hailey's little arms around Daisy's neck was so tempting that she was on the verge of letting Hailey sit in the saddle again when the cell phone in her back pocket buzzed.

A quick look at the display sent her heart rate ratcheting upward. There were no good reasons her neighbor should call. And the bad ones all had something to do with her dad.

Had he set the house on fire? Had he fallen and broken his other leg?

Oh please, don't let it be that.

She put the phone to her ear. "Mrs. Carrington?"

"Amanda, get home quick!" the older woman ordered. "There's a party at your house. Things have gotten out of hand. The noise—it's awful! If you don't put a stop to it, I'll have to call the police."

Well, at least her dad hadn't burned down her house.

Thankful for small favors, Amanda offered quick assurances that she was on her way. She didn't have to tell Mitch that their afternoon had been cut short. He gave her a warm squeeze that sent a flood of longing and hope from her fingertips to her toes.

Grabbing Daisy's reins in one hand, he hefted Hailey onto his hip with the other. "Let's go," he said.

Mitch was already jogging toward the barn by the time Amanda placed a tersely worded phone call to her father. Music blared through the earpiece as she threatened the man with bodily harm if whatever he had going on at her house hadn't ended by the time she got there. She caught up with Mitch halfway to Daisy's stall. Her boots sending tiny clouds of sand into the air, she trotted along beside him.

"What about you-know-who?" Mitch asked, with

a nod to the little girl who clung to his shoulder and laughed, enjoying this new game.

Amanda bit her lip. Dropping Hailey off with Karen was not an option. Her client had mentioned a shopping foray to the outlet malls in Vero Beach.

"She'll have to come along, I guess," Amanda said, though the solution was far from perfect. She had a feeling the next time she saw her father, there'd be fireworks. Her well of patience had already run dry, exhausted on one senseless errand after another. Throwing a party where the police might be involved crossed a line she couldn't condone.

Twenty minutes later, Amanda's fingers coiled into tight fists as she studied the deep tire tracks that gouged the lawn she'd painstakingly planted the previous fall. The splintered posts and the rail that hung drunkenly from the front porch put tears in her eyes. She'd spent the better part of the summer sanding and painting the house. The repairs were sure to wreck her budget. As for her temper, that had already snapped, and she knew she'd been wrong to expose Hailey to such destruction.

A different emotion stirred as she watched the little girl try to straighten the flattened blossoms of a hibiscus bush. Only this morning it had been part of a hedge lining the walkway to her front door.

Amanda squatted beside the child. Carefully, she took the broken flowers from Hailey's fingers. "It's okay," she murmured, despite her own tears.

"Miss Amanda, don't be sad." Hailey's little hands cupped her cheeks. The child peered at her, distress filling her pretty blue eyes. "We'll get new ones."

Amanda blew out a calming breath. Okay, so the little girl could throw a hissy fit better than anyone she'd ever seen, but she did have her sweet moments.

Moments that needed to be channeled and encouraged. And, with brand-new certainty, Amanda knew she wanted to be there to see that happen, to help shape the young woman Hailey was destined to become.

Torn between the desire to read her dad the riot act and the need to comfort and protect the child in her arms, Amanda really had no choice. She chose Hailey. Turning to Mitch, she asked him for what she knew was a huge favor.

"Could you talk to him, please, while I take her inside? She doesn't need to see any of this."

Mitch didn't hesitate. He spun in a half circle, then headed around the house to Tom's trailer. He probably didn't hear the thanks Amanda whispered to his retreating back. As for her unspoken *I love you,* he'd have to have been a psychic to acknowledge her thought.

And for that, Amanda was grateful.

BRINGING ALL HIS legal prowess to bear wasn't something Mitch offered to do for just anyone. But when a guy looked into the face of the woman he loved and saw shadows of fatigue and doubt in her eyes, it stirred an urge to protect and defend. He brushed dust and a few strands of horse hair from his T-shirt. He didn't need the right clothes to set one cantankerous old fool on the path to redemption.

Inside Tom's mobile home, a saddle lay in one corner. It took up a fair amount of space in a living room the size of a postage stamp. Mitch sidestepped it, making quick work of the introductions while he crossed a worn carpet to a tiny kitchen. He leaned against a Formica counter littered with dirty dishes. From this position of strength and power, he turned his best glare on the man who sat, sputtering, on a lumpy sofa.

Right away, Tom whined, "Dusty and the boys were only here for a couple of hours. I don't see why Mandy had to get all riled up about it."

"I think it might've had something to do a neighbor threatening to call the police. Any idea what brought that on?"

No wonder Amanda had seemed anxious and out of sorts ever since her father had landed on her doorstep. It hadn't been enough for Tom to ruin her childhood. Now he seemed bent on destroying the life she'd built in Melbourne.

The man in question blew out a breath. "'Cause I had a few friends in? If you ask me, calling the cops was a might overreactive."

No one had asked Tom, and as far as Mitch could tell, the man didn't warrant an opinion.

"Around here, neighbors watch out for one another. They notice when trucks start tearing up the lawn while the owner's not home. I'm sure they were concerned for Amanda's property."

"Shoot. T'weren't like someone was breakin' in. We wuz just havin' us a good time."

A good time? What was his problem?

Mitch kept his tone civil. "It never occurred to you to entertain your friends in your own place?" He let an all-encompassing gaze sweep the trailer Tom called home.

The man on the couch scowled. "Didn't make no sense to do that. She's got more room." His shoulders slumped. "An' I might have wanted to show off a bit."

"You thought throwing a keg party was the best way to do that?" Mitch refused to let himself be taken in by Tom's sympathetic grimace. Amanda had given her father a place to live when he had nowhere else to go. She deserved to be treated better, and Mitch swore he'd do his best to make that happen.

"Pshaw. T'weren't no keg." Tom waved a hand dismissively. "We just had a few beers and such. Trust me, her grass'll grow back. Mandy's makin' a stink out of a hill of beans."

"That's not the way she sees it." Or him, either, for that matter. "You forgot to mention the porch she'll have to fix, the plants she'll have to replace, whatever else you broke."

"Al'right. Al'right." Tom rooted around in his pockets. "Maybe I did let things get out of hand. I'll tell her I'm…" he paused, drawing out the word "…sor-r-ry. I'll pay for what got broke." He pulled out a thick wad of bills, tossing what had to be thousands of dollars onto the coffee table. "Think that'll cover it? We didn't go inside. Stayed right there on the porch the whole time."

The move stole some of Mitch's momentum. "You have money?"

"That?" Tom pointed to the cash. "That's nothin'. Why else do you think I been haulin' my ass around the country, performin' at every taco stand?" He laughed and threw his hands into the air. "There's good money to be had out there, son. Real good."

Brushing back hair that had fallen onto his forehead, Mitch stared at the fifties and hundreds the man had so carelessly tossed down.

"You know my daughter well, do you?"

He looked up to see Tom eyeing him slyly. Mitch drew himself erect, his shoulders squaring. "We met fifteen years ago at rodeo camp." He paused, wondering if Amanda's dad would even remember the summer he hadn't sent so much as a postcard to his daughter.

Tom only shook his head, a faraway look clouding

his eyes. "Things were tough that year. I lost my wife in a car accident earlier in the spring. I pretty much don't remember anything else for a while." He ran his hand up and down the smooth edges of the crutch perched beside him on the couch. "You should'a seen her on a horse. No one could ride better than Mandy's mom. She looks just like her, y'know. Sometimes I can't hardly look at the girl without thinking about Roseanne."

Mitch rubbed his chin. Maybe there was more to Tom's distance from his daughter than he'd thought. But it didn't let the man off the hook for all the years he'd ignored his only child.

"I know you and your wife were committed to your careers, but did you ever consider giving Amanda a real home? Letting her go to school like a normal kid?"

"She had a home," Tom retorted. "Saw a diff'rent part of the country ever' week. Not many kids can say that. We taught her skills she can make a good livin' off till she's as old as I am. 'Sides, she done real good with them home-school books we got her. A might too good. Now, she don't want nothin' to do with the family business."

A throat-clearing cough signaled the end of Tom's reminiscing. His chin rose. "Maybe we wasn't perfect, but me an' Roseanne, we done out best by that gal. But she don't want nothin' to do with me. I've tried. I can't get anywhere with her."

Sensing a trap, Mitch crossed his arms over his chest and reminded himself to watch out for an ambush. "I'm not sure what you have in mind, Mr. Markette."

"Tom. Call me Tom." With the honest expression of a snake oil salesman, Amanda's father leaned forward. "Mandy, she's got some fool notion she can walk away from the rodeo permanent-like. But it's in her blood.

Same as it's in mine. She'll never be happy with city life."

"I don't know. She seems content to me." The man really didn't know his daughter. She'd left the rodeo scene so long ago the door had shut on her ever returning to it.

"Not for long," Tom countered. "She was practically born with reins in her hand and straw in her hair." He leaned forward, his hand on the heavy plaster cast. "If this leg of mine don't heal right, I'm gonna hang up my spurs. The Markette family business'll be all hers then. She'll need to keep it running, make enough to support us both. She can't do that here."

Mitch fought to keep his mouth shut. The man was delusional if he thought Amanda would give up all she'd accomplished.

But Tom wasn't finished. "After that little rodeo ya'll had, she took up ridin' again. Mark my words." He stabbed the air between them. "She's gonna wake up one of these days and feel the itch to hit the road. I imagine she already has." With a satisfied smirk, he eased back onto the cushions. He propped his broken leg up on the worn coffee table.

"I wouldn't be so sure, Mr. Markette."

For someone who planned to move on, Amanda had put down substantial roots. She'd bought a house and poured her savings into the law office, turning the once run-down building into a showcase. She'd worked hard to establish her practice.

Was she as ready to settle down emotionally? Only time would provide the answer, but aware that Tom's eyes were still on him, Mitch wrenched his thoughts away from the future and focused on the situation at hand.

"Tell me, man to man. Is my girl any good at this legal stuff?"

The question stirred an urge to boast about the woman he loved.

"Amanda has a real gift for family law. She's quite the proponent of children's rights."

"That just goes to prove my point. No one's ever gonna get rich representin' kids." Tom shook his head.

Did the man honestly not understand that *he* was the reason for the choice Amanda had made?

Much as he wanted to ask the question, Mitch held back. He wasn't here to resolve Amanda's long-term relationship with her father. No, that was up to her. But she'd asked him to make it crystal clear to her dad that she wouldn't put up with any more of his shenanigans. Mission accomplished. Still, Mitch couldn't resist giving the old man one final piece of advice.

"Mr. Markette, I'm sure you want what you think is best for Amanda, but she's a grown woman. The time when you or anyone else can tell her how to live her life is over. Now, if you'll excuse me, I'd like to spend some time with my own daughter this afternoon."

With that, Mitch picked up Tom's money and headed for the door, convinced he'd made as much headway as anyone could. Once outside the cramped trailer, though, he couldn't deny that Tom and Amanda's problems had made him think about his relationship with Hailey. Sooner than he liked, she'd start grade school. Before he knew it, she'd be graduating from high school and heading off to college. Someday she'd fall in love, marry, have kids of her own. He intended to be there for her every step of the way. Only to do that, he had to be a part of her life now.

And that meant sharing more time with his little

girl than a few hours Sunday afternoons, didn't it? The answer was a resounding yes. Vowing to make some changes, Mitch crossed the yard to Amanda's back door.

Inside, a curious mix of Spartan and cozy country furnishings made him wonder if Tom didn't know Amanda better than either of them had given him credit for. Mitch passed through an austere kitchen to a dining room where law books and files littered the table. He followed a murmur of voices through a living room filled with creamy leather furniture surrounded by stark white walls. Two gunfighters squared off on the cover of a novel that lay facedown on a sturdy end table. Despite the book and a stack of pillows and neatly folded blankets at one end of the couch, the room had the slightly stale air of disuse.

His feet in motion, he continued down a short hallway to the door standing open at the end. He lingered on the threshold, studying a room where walls the color of sunset on an open prairie made the perfect backdrop for posters from Amanda's rodeo days. Shelves groaned under the weight of all her awards. The enormous gold buckle she'd won in Las Vegas rested in a display case along with more trophies of various colors and shapes than he could count. And in the center of the room, grinning happily, the woman who stirred thoughts of family dinners and cozy evenings at home sat on the floor beside a trunk overflowing with clothes.

Clothes that had nothing to do with the staid, middle-class life of a prosecuting attorney.

Unease built within him as Mitch watched Amanda plunge her hand to the bottom of the chest. Her fingers came up clutching an elaborately sequined shirt and matching leggings. She gave the wrinkled items a quick shake before holding them up.

"Here we go." She smiled at the little girl standing beside her. "I think these might fit. Want to try them on?"

Hailey's eyes grew wide as saucers. She clutched the clothes and spun in a circle.

"Daddy!" She spotted him at the doorway and ran to his side. "Look, Daddy. They're so sparkly!" She tugged his hand, drawing him to the center of a room filled with reminders of the life Amanda had once led, and which, according to her dad, was hers for the asking anytime she wanted.

"Miss Amanda said I can wear them," his daughter breathed. "Can I, Daddy. Can I?"

Mitch wavered only a moment. At his nod, Hailey practically raced down the hall to the bathroom. As soon as she left, he turned to Amanda, bent and dropped his hands on her shoulders. Before they took another step, he had to know where things stood. Was her father right? Was she even now mentally packing her suitcases? If so, he needed to back off. Not only for his sake, but for Hailey's.

"Do you ever miss it?" he managed to ask despite the lump in his throat. "Being on the road, playing to the crowd?"

Amanda sobered. She tipped her face toward his.

"I walked away from all this for a reason." She swept the room with one hand, taking in all the trophies and awards. "This was my dad's dream, my mom's. Not mine. It was a hard life. Always performing, always on the road, never having a place to call your own. One night you're in Tulsa. The next, Pensacola. After a while, the name of the town doesn't matter. It's just one arena after another."

She scrambled to her feet, her eyes never leaving his.

"More than anything, I wanted to go to bed every night knowing I'd wake up in the same city the next morning. And the morning after that."

Mitch's heart pounded in his chest. She was saying all the right things. Hitting all the right buttons. But was he part of the future she envisioned for herself? He had to know.

"Any room for me in that life?"

A smile flirted with her lips and she slipped her arms around his waist. "I'd like that," she whispered.

The moment definitely called for a kiss, but aware his daughter could burst in on them at any moment, Mitch barely let his lips brush Amanda's. He wrapped her in his arms, letting his embrace say the words he couldn't speak, promising the future they both wanted but dared not voice.

All too soon, the squeak of a door and footfalls in the hall drove them apart, but Amanda stayed close, not straying from his side while Hailey marched about the room showing off her new clothes. Later, as he was strapping his child into her car seat, it hit him that Tom Markette was in for a surprise.

Amanda was here to stay.

Certain that she'd made a home in Melbourne, Mitch asked if *he* was the kind of man Amanda deserved. A man who loved her for who she was, not someone he wanted her to become, or someone she once was.

Was he that man?

He wanted to be. He'd never quite fallen out of love with the girl he'd met so many years ago. Now that they'd been given a second chance, he determined to give it his best shot.

Chapter Ten

When the doorbell rang one evening, Mitch looked up from the legal brief spread across his desk. Anticipating his daughter's laughter, he smiled. Reality struck when only silence answered a few dying echoes. He drew in a sharp breath.

What had he been thinking?

Nearly three months had passed since Hailey last giggled and raced him to the front door. He struggled, wincing as the truth whispered through him. He'd never appreciated those times half as much as he should have. Given the chance, he would not repeat that mistake.

He glanced at the calendar, where red ink marked the date he and Karen would face off in Judge Dobson's courtroom. That was the day he'd finally prove his innocence. The day the dark cloud over his name would evaporate. The day he could finally bring his daughter home and put his plan to spend more time with her into action.

The attorney side of him told him not to count on regaining full custody. Dobson had already turned down his motion for an earlier hearing, refusing to consider the testimony that would have put an end to the supervised visitation. If it hadn't meant spending more time with Amanda, Mitch might have railed against the decision. But now that he could prove Hailey's injury had been an accident, it was just a matter of time before the judge acknowledged it, too.

A sharp pounding pulled Mitch out of his reverie. Whoever was standing on his doorstep had clearly run out of patience. Shoving aside the concerns that were never far from his thoughts, he headed for the door.

A glance through the foyer's decorative window banished them completely. The day he'd discovered Amanda was representing his ex-wife, he wouldn't have wasted two cents on a bet that they'd wind up together. Now she played a major role in every possible version of his future. Which made the court date next week doubly important. Once it was behind them, they could finally be together.

Anticipation sent a shiver down his spine.

He hurried to open the door, as surprised by the unexpected midweek visit as he was by his reaction. One good look at Amanda's tearstained face, though, and all thoughts of the future were instantly replaced by concern. Certain he hadn't said or done anything that would cause such angst, he swung the door wide.

"What's wrong?"

She stalked into the house. "Unbelievable. The unmitigated gall of some people is just unbelievable." She waved a handful of tattered papers in the air.

A piece escaped and sailed to the floor at Mitch's feet. Retrieving it, he stared at an advertisement for the county fair. Right away, he spotted the addition to an ad that was already prominently displayed in every store window. In huge bold letters, the flier announced a special appearance of the Markette Ropin' Team to follow the beauty pageant on Saturday night.

With none another than Mandy Markette as the star.

A muscle in his jaw ticked. Despite Amanda's assurances that she was wasn't going anywhere, the idea that she had caved in to her father's demands was far more plausible than Mitch cared to admit. But if she was upset...

"It's not true?" He held his breath, waiting for her answer.

Amanda speared him with an incredulous glance. "Of course not."

Relief washed over him, and his jaw relaxed.

"When you spoke with him Sunday, did he say anything about this?"

Mitch hadn't covered much more than the basics of that conversation. In the days that followed, Amanda had been so busy packing up her father's mobile home and moving him to a trailer park out past Boots and Spurs that they'd hardly spoken.

"He asked if I'd convince you to give up the foolish notion of being a lawyer. I told him you were smarter than that. I guess he didn't listen."

"He's had these plastered all over town." Amanda swiped tears from her cheeks. "I've been taking them down as fast as I find them." She drew a tissue from her hip pocket and wiped her nose. "I don't think I got them all."

She tossed the fliers onto the table behind the couch. Turning, she stood, her hands on her hips. "I just don't get it. All those years, he barely knew I was alive. Now he's trying to run my life."

Mitch hesitated. As much as he dreaded the possibility of losing Amanda, their relationship had to be built on honesty if it was to survive. That meant he had to tell her everything he knew.

"When he and I talked, I got the impression your

dad has regrets. He sees the family business as a way
to forge a relationship with you. You saw the wad of
cash he was carrying around. He says that's just the tip
of the iceberg." Mitch crushed the advertisement she'd
handed him. "Sounds like he's tired of waiting for you
to decide on your own. This—" he aimed the ball toward the nearest trash can and let fly "—must be his
way of pushing you in the direction he wants you to go."

Conflicting emotions warred across her features. Her
fingers fluttered against her chest. With a soft "Oh!" she
slowly sank onto his couch. "Okay, that makes sense
now," she said.

Amanda passed a hand over her face before staring
up at Mitch, her eyes filled with pain. "I went with him
to the doctor's the other day. The news wasn't good. His
prospects of ever riding again—at least to perform—
are somewhere between slim and none."

"That's too bad."

"Yeah, it is." She sighed. "After the rodeo, the Markette team became the most important thing in his life.
I can see why he'd pull something like this if he thought
it was the only way to keep the show going. To have me
in his life. But I'm not that lonely little girl anymore.
The one who'd do anything to get his attention. I've
moved on. He should, too."

She stood and crossed to the farthest end of the room
where she railed against her father for a minute or two
before her head came up. Her jaw firmed. Determina-
tion deepened her voice. "He can find someone else to
take over. Any number of performers would. Royce—
you met him at the Saddle Up Stampede—he'd jump
at the chance."

At last, she turned an imploring look his way. "He

just makes me so angry. Why does he still get to me like this?"

During his stint as a husband, Mitch's advice or help had never been appreciated by his wife. But the woman in his living room was nothing like Karen. Amanda was strong and capable of making it on her own. It as one of the things he admired about her. Deciding that if they were going to have a life together, they had to share the good and the bad, he offered the lesson it had taken him a while to absorb after his marriage fell apart.

"You can tell him how much it bothers you, but there's not much else you can do. You can't control him. Not him or anyone else, for that matter. Your reaction to him, that's what you're in charge of."

He waited, anxious to see whether or not he'd painted a target on his shirt, or if Amanda would agree. The tightness in his chest eased as acceptance dawned in the prettiest green eyes he'd ever seen.

"You're right. You're absolutely right." The stiffness left her shoulders, her anger melting in waves. "I was planning to call the people in charge of the fair tomorrow, anyway. I'll add this to my list. Let them know there's been a mistake. Mandy Markette will *not* be in the show." She shrugged. "I'll talk to Dad, too. Like you said, the rest is up to him."

She paused, eyeing Mitch cautiously, her weight shifting from one foot to the other in a manner that told him something else was on her mind.

"What?" he asked.

"Did you know Karen entered Hailey in the Little Miss Cowgirl contest?"

"She didn't." His stomach rolled at the idea of his daughter parading across a stage with makeup slathered on her face, her hair stiff and piled high.

Amanda's head tilted to one side. "You don't think it's a good idea?"

"A beauty pageant for preschoolers?" Mitch couldn't shake his head fast enough. "What on earth was Karen thinking?"

"Oh, this isn't anything like those programs you've seen on TV," Amanda offered quickly. "It's more like a talent contest. The kids dress up and perform, but the emphasis is on having fun. Karen sees it as a mother-daughter bonding thing more than anything else."

When she put it that way, Mitch could hardly object. Hailey didn't talk about Karen often when he was around, but from the little she did say, he knew his daughter's attitude toward her mother had changed. She no longer pitched a fit when it was time to go home after their Sunday afternoon visits. And several times, she'd mentioned a book Karen had read to her or a game they'd played. Though he would never in a million years choose this way for Hailey to get to know her mom, in the grand scheme of things, he had to admit it was a good idea that they'd grown closer.

Imagining a parade of little girls, each butchering the latest Taylor Swift release, Mitch winced, but knew he'd smile and nod his way through it. "I suppose you're lending her an outfit for the program?"

"Why not?" Amanda shrugged. "Hailey has her act all planned out."

He braced himself. Even at her tender age, his daughter had a knack for standing out from the crowd.

"She intends to ride Daisy in the show."

Mitch had already lifted his hands to signal a stop to such nonsense when Amanda tossed a final ingredient into the mix.

"And rope a steer."

He didn't know whether to laugh or cry. The idea was ridiculous, of course, but he had to ask, "How does she come up with this stuff?"

Laughing along with him, Amanda gestured with open palms. "Who knows? That call I was planning to make? I'm sure live animals aren't allowed onstage, but I thought I'd better get a copy of the rules before she gets her hopes up. Hailey can be pretty insistent."

"Yeah, tell me something I don't know."

He studied Amanda. A subtle shift in the atmosphere told him they'd spent enough time talking about people who weren't in the room. "I was just going to pour myself a glass of wine. Care to join me?"

A warm glow filled her eyes. That was all it took to send him to the kitchen while she made herself comfortable. Fighting a sudden nervous anticipation, Mitch grabbed a crisp chardonnay from the wine rack. He hadn't been out on a date in years. It'd been even longer since the last time he'd spent quality time alone with a woman in the house. Back in the day, when he was young, single and on the prowl, entertaining had been second nature. Now, he had to think about it as he reached past a stack of Tupperware to a serving tray. He dumped crackers into a bowl, tugged a block of cheddar from the fridge.

He wanted nothing more than to get cozy on the couch with Amanda, but held back, determined to let her take the lead. He considered it a good sign when she curled up within touching—if not kissing—distance on the sofa.

While he poured, she asked, "What's the latest between you and the district attorney?"

He feigned interest in the topic and told her what he knew. "He still wants to name me as his replacement. The governor has scheduled a press conference toward the end of next week. He'll announce Randall as his choice for the cabinet post. That should trigger the rest of the dominos, assuming Judge Dobson and Sarah Magarity agree that Hailey's injury was an accident."

Amanda's eyebrows lifted. She chewed on her thumbnail, a sign that something he'd said didn't quite sit right with her. "And you'll take the job?"

"Frankly, I've been so focused on bringing Hailey back home that I haven't given it much thought."

Her hand fell away from her mouth and Amanda shook her head. "There's a lot riding on next week, then. The hearing with Dobson. Your promotion. The custody issue." She twisted a loose strand of hair between her fingers.

Mitch studied her solemn face. "Are you sure you want to talk about this?"

Amanda met his gaze. "I think we've put off talking about it long enough. Besides, I filed my final report with DCF after your last visit with Hailey. Sarah Magarity even called to go over a few points yesterday, so I'm officially done with my supervisory duties until our next court date."

At the social worker's name, Mitch's gaze tightened. He knew he shouldn't, but he had to ask. "Did Magarity give any indication about…"

"About how she was leaning? No. But she asked my opinion so I gave it. I said the same thing I've said all along—that you're a positive influence in your daughter's life."

"Thanks." Mitch exhaled slowly. "Between the witnesses I've lined up and your reports, I'm hopeful Dobson will finally see that Hailey's accident was just that—an accident." Once that was behind him, the judge had to agree Mitch provided the better home for his daughter.

"What will that mean for…" She paused, unable to find the words.

She didn't need to. He knew where she was headed and felt his lips firm, his shoulders square. This wasn't the conversation he'd planned on having over wine and cheese on the one night he and Amanda had together, but she was right. They had to address the elephant in the room.

Bluntly, he tossed his cards onto the table. "I have to do what's best for Hailey."

Concern flashed in Amanda's eyes and she grasped his wrist. "Karen might have started out on the wrong foot, but unlike my dad, she's changed over the past few months. She's doing her best to be a good mom. Are you sure it's in Hailey's interest to take that away from her?"

"That's not what I meant."

Mitch cleared his throat, knowing what he was about to say would come as a shock. It had to. The realization had practically driven him to his knees when he'd finally understood what his heart had been trying to tell him. He cupped his hand over Amanda's.

"Hailey needs both of us—Karen and me—in her life. Our daughter's not some pawn on a chessboard to be captured by the king or the queen. So as much as it'll kill me a little, I'll make sure Karen gets reasonable visitation once this is all behind us."

Amanda's breath caught in an audible gasp. She gazed at him, wonder filling her eyes. "You're sure?"

He managed a quick nod and sipped some wine while she processed the information. He wasn't at all surprised when she asked him for specifics. If their roles were reversed, he'd want to know the same thing.

"Dinner once a week. Visitation every other weekend. An amicable split of the holidays and summers. What do you think?" He slipped his hand under Amanda's until their fingers entwined.

She took a quick gulp from her glass and rubbed one finger across her lips. "It certainly sounds like a good offer."

He brushed aside the fleeting sensation that she was holding something back. Though he'd hoped for her immediate support, it made sense that Amanda would need to run any kind of proposal past Karen before she agreed. Not that his ex was likely to turn this one down. It meant their daughter would spend time with both her parents.

"This way, Hailey wins," he whispered. "And now, enough talk."

He took the wineglass from Amanda's hand and gently set it on the coffee table. Leaning in, he brushed his lips across hers to catch a hint of tangy cheese, dry wine. Combined with her own personal scent, the taste was irresistible. When she slid into his arms, he wanted more than just to explore her mouth, her lips. He wanted to make her his own. And for the first time since they'd met all those months ago at the Saddle Up Stampede, he knew they both envisioned a future together.

She was pressed against him, his fingers tracing the curve of her hip. Her hands, though toughened from years of riding, felt like velvet. Her touch sent shudders unlike anything he'd ever experienced racing across his skin.

He trailed one finger down her rib cage.

"I want our first time to be special." His breath was rough, and he worked to control it. "Not here on the couch like a pair of randy teenagers." He brushed another kiss across Amanda's swollen lips. "Upstairs?" he suggested.

The dreamy look faded from her eyes. Her fingers stroked his jaw. "You don't know how much I want to do exactly that," she whispered.

There was a "but" in there some place. Mitch tried to ignore it and failed.

"But…?"

"But not tonight," she breathed. "We've already pushed the boundaries too far."

"When?" he growled. He put his mind to work grappling with the delay his body didn't want to accept.

"Next Saturday? After the county fair?"

They'd stand on opposite sides of the courtroom one final time two days before the fair.

"Saturday, no matter what."

"Whatever the outcome," she answered.

The words were right, but something in her eyes shifted, and once again he had the feeling she knew more than she was telling. He won the battle against pressing her for an explanation. He trusted this woman with his heart. Whatever she was hiding, she would tell him when she was ready. No matter what her secret was, it wouldn't destroy what they had together.

MITCH PULLED A PEN, a notepad and a stack of files from his briefcase. He organized them quickly on the table at the front of the room, then sat, his chair angled so he could read the faces of those who entered the small courtroom. Not that it did him any good. If the social worker, Sarah Magarity, had an opinion on his case, she hid it well behind a tight-lipped reserve. Joey and Chuck slid into the back row, looking uncomfortable. Mitch couldn't tell which was to blame—the unfamiliar surroundings or their brand-new suits and ties. He tried to catch Amanda's eye, but she and Karen walked in together and immediately sat at the plaintiff's table. Maybe it was his imagination, maybe it was nerves, but something about the set of Amanda's shoulders deepened his anxiety. A single glimpse of Karen's strained features stirred an uneasy suspicion that a nasty surprise stalked his future.

His mouth went so dry he downed half a glass of water while giving himself a stern warning to remain calm. He couldn't react emotionally—whether the threats were real or imagined. Not with Hailey's future at stake. No, the best way to ensure success was to follow his carefully mapped out agenda. First, he'd put an end to the speculation that he'd hurt his child. After that, he'd deal with the custody decision.

Come what may, he meant what he'd said to Amanda earlier in the week. Hailey was more than a set of dishes that should have been divvied up in the divorce decree. He and Karen shouldn't squabble over her as if she were; she needed the security and love of both her parents. He'd do his part to see that she got it. He glanced at his ex-wife and prayed she'd do the same.

The door behind the judge's bench eased open as the bailiff issued the standard line, "All rise for the Honorable Jeffrey Dobson."

Mitch straightened his tie, wrestled his nerves into submission and stood along with the dozen or so others in the courtroom.

"Our first order of business this morning concerns Hailey Goodwin and her parents," Dobson announced after a quick review of the day's docket. "Are all the parties and witnesses in attendance?"

At Amanda's prompt "Yes, Your Honor," the judge swung toward Mitch.

"And are you ready, Counselor?"

The unexpected warmth in Dobson's voice helped Mitch find his feet. While the doors behind him opened and closed to admit a late arrival, his assurance that they could proceed rolled off Mitch's tongue with practiced ease. A ripple of whispers passed through the room, and Dobson gave someone a deferential lift of his chin, but Mitch ignored it all. With his gaze solidly planted on the man who controlled his daughter's fate—and his own—he called his first witness.

He wiped his sweaty brow while Chuck swore to tell the truth, the whole truth. Despite his own pounding heart, Mitch aimed an encouraging smile at the boy. They'd decided that Chuck should tell the story in his own words, so he just said, "Tell us what happened," and stepped aside, the crossed fingers of one hand hidden in his pants pocket.

"There was a lady with two little girls in the park. While the kids played, you—" Chuck nodded at Mitch "—you and the woman talked. When you turned to say goodbye to them, your little girl, she climbed up the monkey bars. Fast, like. You went running over, but just as you got there, she fell off the top bar." He turned an earnest face toward Judge Dobson. "I saw him grab for her. She yelled. Next thing I knew, Mr. Goodwin was shouting did we have a cell phone and yelling for Joey to dial 911."

Dobson leaned forward. "You did great, Chuck," he said, approval turning his solemn voice softer than normal. "I have one question and then we'll let you go. You say Mr. Goodwin ran over to the monkey bars, and Hailey fell just as he got there. You're sure that's exactly the way it happened? He didn't grab her first?"

Pale beneath his freckles, Chuck shook his head. "It happened really fast, but I'm sure. He didn't pull her from the bars or nothing like that. He had to step quick to catch her before she hit the ground."

Mitch drew in a much needed breath. Chuck's account of the events that fateful afternoon should be enough to clear his name. But he wanted more. Wanted to prove beyond a shadow of a doubt that he was innocent. He prepared to call another witness while the young man stepped down from the stand, but Dobson held up one finger. He turned to the redhead seated among the front-row spectators.

"I think I'd like to hear from DCF," he announced.

Mitch choked back a protest at the sudden change of plans. Just because Dobson had returned from vacation a more relaxed version of his old self, that didn't mean crossing him was a good idea. Besides, though Joey was up next, his testimony wouldn't really add much. By his own admission, the boy hadn't seen Hailey fall. He could only corroborate part of Chuck's story. Opting for the safest path, Mitch sank into his chair.

"Your Honor," Sarah Magarity said as soon as she took the stand, "other than this single incident, there are no allegations of neglect or abuse in the Goodwin home. With Mr. Goodwin's permission, I contacted Hailey's pediatrician. He spoke quite favorably about the child…and her father. All the reports we've gathered— our own, as well as those from Ms. Markette—indicate that, until this accident, Mr. Goodwin provided a good home and adequate supervision for his daughter."

The wan smile she aimed at Mitch temporarily lightened the ton of worry he carried on his shoulders. But once the DCF worker stepped down from the witness stand, the tension in the room rose to a palpable level. Dobson's pen made scratching sounds on a pad of paper. The noise echoed through the hushed atmosphere. Minutes stretched into an eternity before he looked up.

"Mr. Goodwin."

"Yes, Your Honor?"

Mitch wished Amanda were sitting beside him. He wanted her hand in his, needed her support. But until they saw this thing through, she was with Karen and he was on his own. There wasn't much he could do but stand there and take it like a man, so he stood.

"Mr. Goodwin, it appears that your daughter's injury was the result of an accident, and that the court owes you an apology. Therefore I'm lifting the requirement for supervised visitation, effective immediately."

The only thing unexpected about the tidal wave of relief that swept over Mitch was its intensity. Though he'd known he was nervous about the outcome, he hadn't expected his legs to buckle beneath him. It was a good thing there was a chair behind him, he thought, collapsing onto it with a heartfelt "Thank you, Your Honor."

In the space of two seconds, before Dobson spoke again, Mitch imagined the over-the-top party he'd throw to welcome his daughter home. Eager to hear how soon that might be, he leaned toward the judge and waited. Instead of making another announcement, the man banged his gavel and ordered a fifteen minute recess. He retreated into his chambers and closed the door.

A shuffle of feet, a rustle of clothing came from the benches. Even knowing he should thank Chuck and Joey for coming, Mitch stayed put. He barely had the strength to swing a glance across the aisle to Amanda's chair. Her face brightened with a congratulatory smile that quickly dimmed, changing into an expression he didn't comprehend until a hand descended on his shoulder.

Mitch caught the flash of a gold Rolex disappearing beneath the sleeve of an expensive Italian suit. Suddenly, the judge's earlier nod to a latecomer made sense. Mitch hauled himself to his feet and shook his boss's hand.

"You probably feel like the weight of the world has lifted." District Attorney Randall Hill spoke in hushed tones quite unlike his usual expansive voice.

"I wouldn't go quite that far. Dobson still has to issue his ruling on permanent custody. But yeah." Mitch added an aw-shucks grin to hide the depth of his relief. "It feels good."

The D.A. was a busy man, too busy to waste time on pointless chatter. He stepped closer, his voice dropping so low Mitch barely heard it.

"Stop by my office when you're done here. We have some details to work out before the press conference. Now that this mess is cleared up, I'll want to name you my successor as soon as possible."

Despite the warm glow Randall's words ignited in his chest, Mitch hesitated. He'd coveted the position of head prosecutor since the day he'd first hung an Officer of the Court badge around his neck. But things had changed over the past three months. Thanks to Amanda, his priorities had shifted. He no longer had the commitment and drive required of a lead prosecutor. To be honest, he wasn't sure he ever would again. But knowing that and admitting it to Randall were two different things. In the end, he hedged, going along with a back-slapping excitement he really didn't feel, and assuring his boss they'd speak later.

Would Amanda understand how much Mitch had changed?

Across the aisle, she sat in whispered conversation with his ex-wife. He couldn't see their faces, but their body language told him Karen and her lawyer were arguing. The sight let loose another qualm of unease. One that only grew after Randall left and Dobson banged his gavel, summoning the courtroom to order. Mitch folded his hands, pressing his fingers together tightly as the judge spoke.

"I'd like to commend everyone on the way they've handled themselves during what I'm sure has been an arduous time."

Though Mitch wished the man would simply get on with it, *hurry* wasn't in Dobson's post-vacation vocabulary. Not as it had been the last time they'd faced one another. Today, he waxed on about the court's duty to protect the best interests of the child before, finally, he turned to Mitch.

"Your daughter's shoulder healed well?"

"Yes, Your Honor," Mitch conceded. "She's back to doing all the things little girls do to give their daddies heart attacks."

A titter of laughter sounded behind him. A vacant smile passed over Dobson's face before he swiveled toward Karen. "Ms. Goodwin, I trust all has gone well with you and your daughter these past few months?"

Karen cleared her throat. Sounding much more sure of herself than she had that first day in court, she answered smoothly, "Yes, Your Honor. Hailey is a delightful child. I'm blessed to have her in my life."

"No changes in your request for custody?"

From the corner of his eye, Mitch caught movement. He thought Amanda started to say something, but before she could get a word out, Karen's hand sliced through the air. When Amanda eased back in her chair, whatever she'd been about to say silenced by her client, Mitch instinctively braced himself.

"Well, there is one thing…." Karen smiled prettily up at the judge.

A frown deepened the lines on Dobson's face. "And what would that be?"

"Your Honor, the store where I work, Bella Designs, is opening a new branch in Miami. I've been asked to run it. I'll need to be on-site when construction starts in a week. Would that change things?"

As the meaning of Karen's question sank in, Mitch felt the ground beneath his feet shift. His heart pounded as if it might hammer its way out of his chest. This was the secret Amanda had kept from him? The reason for the vague answers, the disquieted looks that had bothered him the past couple of weeks? This was no small secret. No courtroom strategy to be safeguarded from an opponent. It was betrayal, pure and simple, and he felt its sharp edge knife deep into his heart.

Sour laughter rolled through him. He bit it back, considering the unbelievable irony of the situation. Here he was, turning down the crowning jewel of his career in order to concentrate on his family, while Karen had accepted a promotion that would effectively end her day-to-day involvement in their daughter's life. Unless…

He swallowed, his muscles ratcheting so tight he could scarcely breathe as Dobson punched keys on his laptop. Mitch waited while the judge ran a finger across the screen. Mitch thought the lack of oxygen might make him pass out by the time Dobson said the words any first-year law student knew by heart.

"As long as Florida remains your primary residence,

Ms. Goodwin, I see no reason why your move to Miami should have an impact on this case. That being said, I'd like to proceed."

This time, when Dobson turned toward him, Mitch fought disbelief at the sadness in the old man's face.

"Mr. Goodwin, I'm sure you've provided a wonderful home for your daughter. By all reports, you've been a model father." The man on the bench exhaled a heavy sigh. "But, call me old-fashioned, I still think a young girl should be with her mother whenever possible. So, in the matter of the minor child Hailey Goodwin, this court awards permanent custody to the plaintiff."

Mitch stared at a world filled with laws and points of order and rules that no longer made sense. Not when a happy little girl could be torn from the only home she'd ever known, and sent to live in another part of the state with a mother she barely knew. A roaring sound filled his head. It all but drowned out the judge's instructions concerning child support and visitation. Mitch dropped his head onto his hands, devastation washing over him in gut-wrenching waves.

He was vaguely aware that across the aisle Amanda and Karen were engaged in a quiet but heated argument. Mitch fought his way to his feet as a while-hot anguish threatened to send him to his knees. Nausea rolled through him and the bands across his chest spread into his throat, tightening until the only word he could manage was a harshly whispered "No."

Behind him, people grabbed purses and briefcases, heading for the door the moment Dobson adjourned the court. It didn't matter. None of it did. Only two things mattered—Hailey and Amanda. He'd lost both of them.

The betrayal of one had cost him the other.

Chapter Eleven

"This court awards permanent custody to the plaintiff."

Amanda sucked in a breath. Half expecting Mitch to come flying across the courtroom—at the judge, at her, at Karen—she braced for an explosive outburst. When dead silence replaced the expected angry torrent, she sent a searching glance toward the man she loved.

He sat in stony silence behind the defendant's table.

As Dobson banged his gavel, setting his decision in stone, Mitch swayed. His shoulders slumped and he leaned forward on arms braced against the table. Pain radiated from his every pore, making him look for all the world as if he'd been dealt a mortal blow.

He was beaten, and everyone in the room knew it.

Amanda longed to reach out, to stand beside him, to lend him enough of her own strength to get them past the shock he hadn't seen coming.

She couldn't move.

Trapped, held prisoner to the decorum of the legal system, she did what was expected of her and dredged up a tremulous version of her victory smile. The bailiff announced a recess, and the judge disappeared into his chambers. His absence set loose a wave of chatter that spread from wall to wall.

Beside her, Amanda felt Karen tremble and wondered why. The woman had achieved exactly what she'd set out to do—she'd wrested custody of her little girl from the man who had raised her. On top of that, she had the judge's blessing to relocate a couple hundred miles farther south. If anything, Amanda's client should be overjoyed.

Yet, shaking like a newborn filly, Karen grasped her arm, a look of puzzled confusion in her hazel eyes. "He does realize what this means, doesn't he? Hailey will have to move away from her friends. Change schools. She'll hardly be able to see Mitch. Dobson will allow that?"

Behind them, footsteps pounded up the aisle.

Amanda didn't have time or energy to spend on a client who'd just been given everything she'd ever asked for, and more. Desperate to get to Mitch, she stuffed papers into her satchel and headed after him, glancing at Karen over her shoulder. "He just did."

Risking her neck, Amanda raced down the corridor on her high heels. She barely managed to glimpse inside the elevator before the doors slid shut. No Mitch. She spun toward the stairwell and the only other possible exit. Her glance over the rail revealed nothing, but someone was quickly climbing the steps above.

"Wait," she called. "Mitch, wait up."

His feet thundered on the stairs, each step taking him farther away from her. Amanda kicked off her heels and ran to the next landing, where she found him waiting, one foot angled toward flight. Unease whispered through her as she saw the hard lines of his face, the dull steel in his eyes.

"Where are you going?" she asked with a breathlessness that had nothing to do with rushing after him and everything to do with fear.

Mitch's gaze slid up the stairs. "The district attorney's office. He wants to discuss my future." Biting sarcasm accompanied his grimace. "I guess I should be grateful that I have a future…with him."

But not with me? Her heart skipped a beat.

"Oh, Mitch," she said, reaching out for him. "I'm so, so sorry." Now that they were alone, she could finally let him see that she was as crushed by the judge's decision as he was.

He flinched away from her touch, his focus locked on a spot over her left shoulder. Jaw rigid, he ground out words. "Congratulations, Counselor. I hope you're proud of what you've done."

His anger stung. She stumbled back a step.

"Please don't make this personal," she pleaded. Words of reassurance filled her heart. She would resign as Karen's attorney. She'd help him appeal Dobson's ruling. Together, they'd win custody of Hailey and have the future they'd planned.

One look at Mitch's face and the words died in Amanda's mouth.

"What choice do I have?" he sneered. "Or wasn't that you standing beside my ex-wife, helping her rip away the one person who held any meaning in my life?"

His words pierced Amanda's heart like bullets. She threw her hands up in defense. Mitch had every right to be angry, to feel hurt, even betrayed. But to lash out at *her?* She wasn't the one who'd decided to take his daughter and move to Miami.

She tasted the heat of an angry response and bit it back, forcing herself to give him some extra leeway. He'd just been dealt a terrible blow. They both had, and she felt his pain. She was nearly sick over it.

"This wasn't the outcome I expected, Mitch, but let

me approach Karen for you. There was a time when she didn't want you to have anything to do with Hailey, but she's changed over the past three months. She's a different person than she was then. I'm sure she'll agree to the same visitation you planned on giving her."

Mitch's laughter, dark and bitter, filled the stairwell. "How the hell am I supposed to have dinner with Hailey on Wednesday nights if she lives in Miami? Or make it to those 7:00 a.m. soccer practices on weekends? Did your client consider that? Did the judge?"

Amanda exhaled. "I was as surprised by Dobson's decision as you were."

"But you knew about Karen's plans. You knew she wanted to uproot my daughter and move three hours away." Mitch's voice dropped an octave. "And you didn't tell me."

He hadn't asked a question, only stated a fact she couldn't refute. Amanda blinked, no longer able to meet his harsh glare. He was right. She had known. She'd feared his reaction from the moment Karen had confided in her.

"How could you keep that a secret?" Biting and caustic, the words hissed from his lips. "After all we've meant to each other, how could you betray me like that?"

Amanda pressed a protective hand to her chest. "I couldn't tell you. But I did my best to warn you."

"You never said one word…"

Amanda winced at the sharp, accusatory tone. The urge to give as good as she got rose. "Oh, but I did," she pointed out. "The day we had the cookout at your house. When I said we couldn't discuss legal strategies with each other, you had to suspect something. You're a smart guy."

Mitch recoiled as if she'd struck him. "That was... *weeks* ago." His gaze dropped to the floor. Slowly, he shook his head. "How could I have been so stupid? I let myself believe you actually cared for me."

Amanda stepped forward. "I did. I—I do. You, of all people, should understand what was at stake. Attorney-client privilege is at the foundation of our legal system. If I broke it, the bar association could strip away my license."

"Better the court should strip away my daughter?" Like a wild horse attempting to throw its rider, Mitch tossed his head. "I'd never keep something like that from you."

Easy for him to say. He wasn't representing Karen.

"She's my client. There were things I couldn't tell you."

"You would have..."

Praying he wouldn't say what she knew was coming next, Amanda braced herself.

"...if you cared for me."

Amanda gave him the only answer she had in her arsenal. "And if you really felt the same way, you wouldn't expect me to."

The truth hurt more than she'd thought possible. Surprisingly dry-eyed for someone who had just realized the man of her dreams didn't live up to reality, Amanda decided that this time she'd be the one to walk away. Turning her back on Mitch and their future, she retraced her way down the stairs. At the second floor landing, she slipped her shoes back on, giving him a final chance to come after her. When he didn't, she stepped from the stairwell into a life that no longer included her first love, the man she'd thought would stand by her no matter what.

Of all the people she didn't want to deal with, Karen was number one on the list. But her client stood, weight shifting from one foot to the other, in the corridor outside Dobson's courtroom. The instant Amanda emerged from the stairs, the frantic woman fairly flew across the carpeted hallway.

"I need to find Mitch. Have you seen him?"

It was a day for surprises, and the breathless question was more of the same. Blindly, Amanda pointed toward the staircase behind her.

Karen lurched past, then spun around to face her. Concern creased her brow and bowed her lips. "Amanda, are you all right?" Her gaze traveled to the door to the stairs and her expression smoothed. "Oh. Is there something going on between you two?"

"I thought there might be, but…" She shrugged. Now that it was over there was no sense pretending. "I was wrong."

A spark of irritation flashed in Karen's eyes before it quickly faded. "Well, you won our case. That's the important thing." She cocked a hip and gave Amanda a quick pat on the shoulder. "You're a better lawyer than I thought." On that note, she ducked into the stairwell.

Barely holding on to her shredded dignity, Amanda blinked to keep her tears at bay. The win was the biggest of her career, but at what cost? She'd lost the love of her life, and Mitch had lost his daughter. Sobs choked Amanda's throat. She swallowed them. "Not here, not now," she breathed, anxious to reach the privacy of her car, her house. Stepping into the empty elevator, she swiped at her wet cheeks.

How MUCH MISERY was a man supposed to take?

Mitch couldn't say for sure, but he had an idea that

losing his daughter and being betrayed by the woman he
loved qualified as more than he was supposed to shoulder. His eyes filled and he scrubbed at his face with the
palms of his hands. His bones ached with such despair
that he craved solitude.

To growl or howl—he wasn't sure which. Maybe
both.

An unavoidable meeting with the district attorney
loomed, but the second it ended, he'd head for home.
There, he'd lick his wounds in private before he figured
out what to do about Hailey.

But he would do something.

Maybe, just maybe, he could have handled losing
custody as long as Karen remained in Melbourne. He
wouldn't have liked it. Well, that was an understatement, wasn't it? He'd have hated it. Hadn't he vowed
to spend more time with his child? Still, he might have
accepted the situation…providing he saw his daughter
regularly. Karen's selfish plan would put two hundred
miles between them. He'd be lucky if he saw Hailey
once a month.

As for Amanda…his anger burned too hot to even
think about her.

"Mitch? Mitch, are you up there?" Karen's shrill
voice echoed up the stairwell.

"Now what?" Groaning, he pushed himself away
from the wall. Down below, he caught a flash of red
heading in his direction. He mopped his face and
wished he'd made it to the safety of the prosecutor's
office before Karen found him.

She continued to climb, her voice rising over the tapping of her heels against the stairs.

"Boy, that sure as heck didn't go the way I thought it
would. Dobson is a stodgy old coot, isn't he? A womb

trumps all—what kind of b.s. is that? He sure pulled a fast one on all of us." She yammered on, without making any sense, until she reached the landing.

Mitch expended every ounce of control to shutter his face. Refusing to look at the woman whose secret plans had destroyed his life, he managed to mutter, "I think you've taken all you can get from me, Karen. There's nothing left."

His ex-wife twisted a rope of pearls between her fingers. "I don't want to take anything. In fact…" She left him hanging while she drew in a breath and exhaled slowly. "I want to give something back."

He risked a glance at the face he'd once been able to read as easily as a newspaper. Karen didn't look jubilant. In fact, unless she'd changed more than he thought anyone could, dismay glistened in her eyes. He listened closer.

"Every person in that courtroom was supposed to be looking out for Hailey. Doing what was best for her. But they were wrong. Dobson was wrong." Several strands of hair a darker shade than he remembered escaped Karen's stylish bun. She shoved them back in place. "It's not fair to uproot her again, take her away from all her friends, her school."

"If you're looking for an argument, Karen, you're talking to the wrong person."

"I never in a million years expected Dobson to award me custody of our daughter. I was sure he'd change his mind if I told him I was moving."

Mitch blinked. Had he heard her correctly? He held his breath, afraid one wrong word, one false move on his part might douse the faint ray of hope that broke through the gloom of an otherwise horrendous day.

"Our daughter is a wonderful little girl, Mitch.

You've done a marvelous job raising her." Karen's voice faltered. She cleared her throat. "She should… she should stay where she belongs. With you."

Mitch's vision swam. Unable to believe what he was hearing, he reached for the wall behind him.

"Of course, I want something in return."

"Anything," he breathed, willing to mortgage the house, sell his car, empty his savings accounts if it meant having Hailey home again.

"Ample visitation. Two weeks in the summer. We can alternate Christmas and Thanksgiving."

The offer was exactly what he'd been prepared to give her. "That sounds more than fair," he said, amazed when his voice didn't break.

"Plus I'll be making frequent trips between Miami and the home office. I'll want to see Hailey whenever I'm in town."

Praying it wasn't a deal breaker, Mitch hesitated. "As long as it doesn't interfere with school and her other activities."

Karen shot him a tight, self-important smile. "Don't worry. I won't turn into a demanding ex-wife like the ones on those nighttime soaps."

She'd already covered that ground, but he bit back the urge to point it out to her.

"Dinner or a girls' day out on Saturday afternoon will be fine." Karen broke eye contact. She studied the floor at his feet. "I think we can dispense with the whole issue of child support, don't you?"

"What?" Mitch feigned surprise. "You aren't going to pay?" He ducked when Karen's fist lightly tapped his upper arm.

"You always were a kidder," she retorted, her chuckle dispelling the tension that filled the stairwell.

Mitch eyed his ex-wife. The question of child support had touched a nerve. Though he never asked a witness a question without knowing the answer ahead of time, Karen wasn't on the stand. And after all she'd put him and Hailey through, he deserved to know what motivated her.

"I thought child support was the reason you wanted Hailey in the first place. Was I wrong?"

His ex-wife's mouth twisted. "I'm not particularly proud of it, but yeah, that was part of my reason for coming back to Melbourne. To tell the truth, it was the main reason I went after custody." She sighed. "Amanda set me straight. Made sure I knew the score early on. By then, well... Once I got to know our daughter, things changed. I changed."

"I'm still confused." Mitch ran a hand through his hair. "Why'd you pursue custody if you weren't going to keep Hailey?"

Karen inhaled deeply, her face softening into feminine lines. "I couldn't let my daughter grow up thinking I didn't want her." Moisture gathered in her eyes. She blinked, and tears spilled onto her cheeks. "A little girl needs to know her mama loves her."

"I told her you did." Though his voice cracked, Mitch insisted on getting the words out. "Every day."

"It's not the same," Karen sniffed. Reaching into the purse that dangled from one slim wrist, she whipped out a tissue, blotted her eyes, then blew her nose in a ladylike fashion. "I'd really like Hailey to stay with me until after the Little Miss Cowgirl contest on Saturday. You are coming to that, aren't you?"

So overwhelmed he could barely whisper the words, Mitch agreed. "I wouldn't miss it for the world."

"Good. Hailey can't wait for you to see her in her

costume. She's been practicing the rope tricks Amanda taught her. Our little girl is so talented, she's sure to win first place. I'll pack up her things and drop her off Sunday afternoon. Unless you have other plans?"

"If I did, I'd cancel them." Nothing short of a category 5 hurricane would keep him from standing in their foyer when Hailey rang the doorbell.

Karen started back the way she'd come, thought better of it and turned to face him. "I don't suppose you'd let me keep Esme, would you? She might like Miami."

Mitch managed a smile. "You'd have to ask her, but I think she and Hailey are a package deal."

"Yeah, that's what I was afraid of." Karen frowned. "I'm sure going to miss that woman."

After his ex-wife traipsed down the stairs and out of sight, Mitch stood for a moment, trying to regain his footing in a world that had tilted back onto its axis. He reached for his phone, eager to share the good news of Karen's change of heart with the one person who would know how much it meant to him. His fingers brushed the hard plastic case, but realizing he had no one to call, he shoved the phone deeper into his pocket.

Okay, so miracles did happen and Hailey was coming home.

But it'd take more than a miracle to resolve things with Amanda.

Chapter Twelve

Amanda gave her reflection in the full-length mirror a once-over.

Puffy eyes reddened by a two-day crying jag stared back. She skimmed down the plain white T-shirt she wore over loose-fitting jeans. Not her best look, she admitted, thrusting her feet into her second-best pair of boots. Still, a definite improvement over the threadbare pajamas she'd worn since staggering into the house beneath the weight of her broken heart.

She'd sworn she'd never get involved with someone who chose his career over his family. And yet she had. Though she'd represented her client to the very best of her abilities, she'd crossed an ethical line by getting involved with Mitch. Not that it had done her any good. The man she'd loved for fifteen years, and lost in fifteen minutes, had marched from a devastating courtroom appearance straight into the District Attorney's office. He'd stopped on his way up the staircase to success only long enough to say they had no future. How could he even think about accepting the huge promotion so soon after losing his daughter...or her?

She should probably hate him for that.

And she would...if all the blame was his. Brushing a hand through her hair, Amanda acknowledged that she'd had her own part to play, and she'd played it well. She'd kept Karen's secret. She couldn't help that Mitch felt betrayed by her actions. Unlike him, she hadn't had a choice.

With a shaky sigh, Amanda plopped a worn cowboy hat over her curls and grabbed her keys, ready for a change of scenery. For something new and different… such as a life without Mitch. Though her mouth trembled whenever her thoughts strayed toward the tall, good-looking attorney, she thought she might be past the worst of their breakup.

Sure, she still had her moments. Moments when she recalled Mitch's kisses or the brush of his long fingers against her jaw. Times when she caught a whiff of his scent as she moved from the couch to the kitchen for another box of tissues.

Keys in hand, Amanda stopped.

Who was she kidding? She wasn't over Mitch. She probably never would be. But she absolutely would not spend the rest of her life pining for a man who didn't love her. And Mitch never had. He'd said as much in the stairwell.

"…the one person who held any meaning in my life…"

Well, he hadn't been referring to her.

This time when she wiped her cheeks, her fingers remained dry. There'd be no more tears. No dreams of a future that was never meant to be.

She'd promised to cheer for Hailey in the Little Miss Cowgirl contest. And unlike a certain tall, handsome lawyer, she kept her promises.

Especially now that Karen was leaving again, just when Hailey was getting to know her mother.

Shaking her head, Amanda thrust a stubborn curl behind one ear. Oh, how she wished that woman had never darkened her office doorway. Karen had brought nothing but needless pain into the lives of everyone around her. If it hadn't been for the brassy blonde...

Her thoughts veering toward a cliff, Amanda hauled up on the reins. As much as she wanted to pin the responsibility for everything that had gone wrong these last three months on Karen, the woman had her good points. The prodigal mom had at least forged a bond with her daughter. Her custody suit had given Mitch the chance to see how important Hailey was in his life. He'd squandered that opportunity by stepping into the D.A.'s shoes, but that wasn't Karen's fault. It was his.

Her emotions back under control, Amanda decided she *was* making progress. She wasn't sure she was strong enough to face Mitch again, but in a town the size of Melbourne, they were bound to run into each other eventually. Why not get it over with?

An hour later, she joined the crowds flocking to the county fair at Wickham Park. While palm fronds waved in a crisp evening breeze, the smells of an old-fashioned carnival perfumed the air. Screams echoed through the darkening sky as cars rocketed along the metal tracks of a fast-moving roller coaster. Delighted cries rose from youngsters strapped securely into large spinning cups.

Last week, Amanda had looked forward to the fair. She'd planned to hold Hailey's hand as they browsed through the animal tents where 4-Hers proudly demonstrated their blue ribbons. With Mitch's arm solidly around her waist, she would have joined the friends and families jamming the wide aisles between displays of homemade jams and cakes. Amanda had dreamed of finally sharing a ride on the Ferris wheel with him.

But not tonight.

Tonight, the exhibits held as much interest as a bag of oats. For all she cared, the hot dog she bought from a vendor could have been made of sawdust. She dumped it into a trash can after one bite.

She blinked back a rogue tear when a young couple strolled past, heads nearly touching as they shared freshly roasted cashews from a paper cone. Afraid her misery would seep through if she saw another pair of young lovers trading bits of wispy cotton candy and kisses in the shadows along the midway, Amanda hurried to the tent designated for the talent show. She ducked through the canvas doorway and scoured the rows where moms and dads, grandparents and the occasional unlucky cousin sat in folding chairs on the bare dirt. Spotting a photographer from the local paper, Amanda imagined Hailey's picture on the front page and, for the first time in days, felt the beginnings of a smile.

It lasted until a glimpse of dark hair sent her mind reeling.

Mitch?

Her chest constricted. For a moment, she couldn't breathe.

Finally, her muscles eased and she told herself she had nothing to worry about. The county's lead prosecutor certainly wouldn't have time for carnivals and fairs, would he?

The realization put her mind, if not her heart, at ease.

An unexpected wave of nervous energy swept her when the program started. Despite her efforts to appear calm and collected for Hailey's sake, she chewed a fingernail as one by one, a parade of children sang or danced across the makeshift stage. When one unfortunate child blanked out completely and stood in thumb-sucking silence until the buzzer sounded, Amanda switched to another nail and worried it to the quick. She'd been pretty sure her heart wasn't working anymore, but there it was, thumping ever faster when Hailey's name was called.

Hailey walked to center stage as if she owned it. She gave the sweetest little curtsy and, while Amanda held her breath, twirled a rope as though she'd been born with it in her hand. The consummate performer, she beamed at the end of her sixty seconds and graciously accepted the trophy for Miss Congeniality. She even remembered to blow kisses as she toddled into the wings.

Amanda caught one and cheered.

Moments later, the contestants swarmed out into the audience. Her applause faltered when she glanced down the row and saw Hailey in Mitch's arms. Right away, Amanda knew she was in trouble. If she'd thought she was over him, being within twenty feet of the man proved how wrong she'd been. Her pulse shifted into a fast trot as she struggled to remember all the reasons he was wrong for her. Okay, maybe she had loved him ever since that summer in Wyoming, but they had grown into adults. With different goals. Different drives. She closed her eyes and pushed her regrets away.

Summoning the courage and bravado that had gotten her through countless rodeo performances, Amanda pried herself out of her chair. Though it made her heart ache to stand so close to him, she listened as Mitch congratulated his daughter on her performance. When Amanda's smile threatened to become a rigid mask, she sipped air through tight lips while Hailey told him all about her trophy.

"It means I'm the nicest!" The child beamed.

At last, the little girl's bubbling account tapered off.

"Sweetheart," Amanda said, "I have to run, but I wanted to say congratulations. You did a great job up there." She motioned toward the stage.

"Did you see, Miss Amanda? Did you see me twirled the rope? I did it just like you showed me."

"You were perfect, sweetie." The child's excitement was so contagious, Amanda couldn't help but feel proud of her. "And what a wonderful trophy." She hefted the shiny plastic cup. "You'll probably have a million of them soon." Unable to resist a little dig, she added, "Make sure your daddy takes the time to build a shelf for you to put it on."

It served Mitch right when he winced.

Hailey tipped her head until she looked straight into Amanda's eyes. "Next time, I'm going to get a bigger one. Can you show me some new tricks, Miss Amanda? How 'bout on Sunday when we go see Daisy?"

Why hadn't she realized that breaking up with Mitch meant breaking up with his daughter, too? Amanda gulped. She wanted to sweep the little girl into her arms and give her hugs and kisses. Wanted to tell her that she'd teach her everything she needed to know, that they'd go shopping and horseback riding together, that one day she'd help her buy a dress for the prom.

But she couldn't. Instead, she needed to speak the hardest word she'd ever say. She needed to tell Hailey no. Her mouth refused to cooperate.

Great.

The favorite word of every two-year-old, and Amanda couldn't utter it. She needed help and sent a pleading look toward the one man who could provide it.

Anguish colored Mitch's eyes a misty blue. Despite it, he cleared his throat.

"Hailey, let's worry about that another day, all right?

Tonight, your mom's going to take you on some of the rides to celebrate." He lifted the little girl so high she squealed. "Sound good?"

Hailey's laughter filled the rapidly emptying tent. While Mitch distracted his daughter, Amanda grabbed a tissue from her purse. Quickly, she blotted her tears. By the time she looked up again, Karen had joined them from the area designated for stage moms.

"You were wonderful, darling." She fell to her knees in front of Hailey and swept her into a hug. "Now, who's ready for some cotton candy and a ride on the merry-go-round?"

Giggling and happy, Hailey jumped up and down yelling, "Me! Me!"

A quiet admonition accompanied the strip of red ride tickets Mitch handed to his ex-wife. "Not the Ferris wheel. Or the roller coaster." He waved a waist-high line through the air. "She's too little."

Surprisingly agreeable, Karen patted Hailey's hand. "No problem. We'll still have tons of fun." She pinned Amanda with a look. "Unless you want me to stay?"

The old Karen wouldn't have even noticed the tension between us.

Amanda thanked her, but insisted her ex-client enjoy the evening with her daughter. Though her brow furrowed, Karen agreed and, reminding Mitch she would drop Hailey off the next day, she stood. Hand in hand, mother and daughter joined the throngs outside the tent, leaving Amanda to stare wistfully after them.

"Thanks," she whispered the moment she and Mitch were alone.

She made the mistake of looking at him. Hope and longing played across his face like shadows. She saw how much he wanted her in the slight tremble of his fingers as he reached for her. She wanted him, too, but wanting and loving were two different things. Unwilling to settle for one without the other, she backed away. Her spine stiffened, and she summoned a smile.

"Sounds like everything has worked out well. Everyone accomplished all they set out to do. Karen has the relationship she's always wanted with Hailey. The phone at my office is ringing off the hook with new business. Your daughter's coming home." Petty didn't become her, so Amanda held back, refusing to mention the fact that Mitch's new job would keep him too busy to enjoy Hailey's company. "It's a good way to leave things, don't you think?"

Under the circumstances, she couldn't quite manage her trademark smile. Deciding a wavering version would have to do, she stuck out her hand. "I wish you all the best."

Mitch's gaze traveled the length of her arm. He stared at her fingers, not grasping them for so long she thought he'd refuse. At the last moment he wrapped his hand around hers. "We promised we'd be together once the custody decision came down. We said no matter what."

Amanda swallowed. "You expected me to choose between my client and you. That choice wasn't mine to make."

Mitch groaned and ran his free hand over his face. "When I thought Karen was taking Hailey to Miami, I said some things I didn't mean. Words I regretted the instant I said them."

"Thanks." Amanda straightened. "I guess we both said things we shouldn't have. But I can't hold you to your promise. That was before."

Mitch's head canted to one side. "Before what?"

She glanced over his shoulder to make sure they had

the tent to themselves. "Before I found out you didn't love me," she whispered.

"Wh-what are you talking about?"

"You made it clear when we spoke in the stairwell. You don't love me. You never did."

"I never said that, Amanda. I wouldn't." He still held her hand in his, and he drew her close enough to cup her fingers over his heart. "I do love you, Amanda Markette. I intend to spend the rest of my life proving it to you. If you'll let me. If you'll give us another chance."

If he loved her, then maybe there was hope....

She closed the door on the lie that would simply lead to more heartache. As clearly as she could see them sitting in rocking chairs on her front porch in their nineties—as much as she wanted that dream to come true—she'd played second fiddle to a man's career most of her life. She wouldn't spend the rest of it trying to prove to another man she was worthy of love. Not even Mitch. She retrieved her fingers from his grasp and stepped back, desperate to put some distance between them.

Determined that there'd be no tears, no recriminations, she said the only words she could. "I love you, too, Mitch. But sometimes love just isn't enough."

Strong feelings played across Mitch's face before they settled into something she chose to believe was resigned acceptance.

"Friends, then?" he asked cautiously.

Disappointed that he'd given in so easily, she refused to acknowledge the longing that swept through her at the memory of how they'd nearly ended up in each other's arms the last time he'd asked that question. This time, she refused to be swayed. They'd part as friends, but this was goodbye.

"Sure," she said, with mixed emotions. "No hard feelings. No regrets."

She read the hesitation in Mitch's eyes, heard it in his voice when he said, "I have lots of regrets, Amanda. Most of them I'll have to learn to live with." He waved a hand. "There's one we don't have to carry with us, though. If you're willing, that is."

Curious, she glanced up at him.

"One spin on the Ferris wheel…for old time's sake?" he asked.

DID THEIR LOVE MEAN SO little to her that she was willing to throw it away?

Every couple fought. Tempers flared. Words that should never have been spoken were uttered in the heat of anger. After you licked your wounds and cooled off, you remembered why you'd fallen in love. You did whatever was necessary to get back in the good graces of the one who made life worth living. No one called it quits over one disagreement.

No one, apparently, except Amanda.

Granted, they'd faced serious problems. From day one, nothing about their relationship had been easy. After the custody hearing, Mitch had been so hurt that he'd struck out, blamed her. But she'd only been doing her job. And when he stopped long enough to think about it, he'd been proud of her for that.

So why, when he was willing to forgive and forget, was she so insistent on calling it quits?

She couldn't be right about them. He refused to believe they'd found one another after all these years only to lose each other again. The past few days— days when Karen's abrupt change of heart should have made him the happiest man on the planet—he couldn't get Amanda out of his head. No matter where he turned, she haunted him.

He'd broken out the grill, thinking to bury his heartache in a good steak and a six-pack. But consumed by memories of his golden girl and the picnic they'd shared with Hailey, he'd tossed the untouched meal into the trash can. He'd upended the full bottle of beer in the sink, sending every mind-deadening drop of liquid down the drain.

He'd tried to catch up on his reading, but the couch where they'd kissed was off-limits. Along with his deck. His car. Boots and Spurs. In short, every place he'd seen Amanda, held her close, heard her laughter. He'd called in sick, something he hadn't done since the last time Hailey brought the flu home from preschool. Tending to his heartache, Mitch had hunkered down in his bedroom, the one place in his house Amanda had never seen…no matter how much he'd wanted to take her there.

He'd come to the fair tonight prepared to make up, to apologize, to get them back on track. Now, searching the green eyes of the woman he'd loved ever since he was a scrawny teenager on a dude ranch in Wyoming, he held his breath and prayed like he'd never prayed before. His heart told him this was his last chance to make things right between them. Without hesitation, he pulled out all the stops.

"One spin on the Ferris wheel…for old times' sake?"

He knew she'd remember the night they'd hitched a ride into town to see her father perform in a small-time rodeo. Afterward, they'd hung out at a carnival much like this one. Hoping for a kiss when they reached the top, Mitch had bought tickets on the Ferris wheel. The ride had broken down just as they were about to board,

but he'd kissed her anyway, and they'd been insepara-
ble after that.

Reminding her of the night they'd shared that first
tentative kiss… It was sentimental and sappy, and some
might even call it cheating. But if he was going to win
Amanda's heart, he couldn't afford to play by the rules
she'd set.

Something glinted in her eye. A spark? A tear? It
didn't matter as long as she gave him time to plead
his case.

"Okay…" she said slowly. "One ride. As long as
when it's over we part as friends." Her voice dropped.
"And nothing more."

He hoped she'd forgive him for bending the truth,
just this once.

As they walked down the midway, he did his best
to comply with her wishes. Despite arms that ached to
snug her to him, he kept his distance. Catching a glim-
mer of sorrow on her face, he resisted the urge to reach
out to her. The line stretched endlessly around the Ferris wheel, but he avoided all talk of what they'd meant
to each other, their hopes, their dreams for the future.
Instead, he filled the time with mindless chatter.

"I saw Royce in the exhibition earlier tonight," he
said when he'd exhausted his supply of topics and they
were still three couples away from the head of the line.
"I guess that means you worked things out with Tom?"

Amanda resettled her cowboy hat. "Now that Dad
can't perform anymore, Royce has joined the Markette
Team."

"Oh?" This was news. Mitch wondered why she
hadn't mentioned it earlier. It took him a second to remember that they hadn't been on speaking terms for
several days.

She shrugged. "Dad got the official word from his doctor last week. I was going to tell you after the custody hearing, but…"

She didn't need to say any more. Mitch knew all too well why that conversation hadn't taken place.

"What's the old buzzard going to do now?" he asked. Though Amanda's voice carried no hint of the tension usually associated with her father, he wanted her to know she could count on him to run interference whenever necessary.

"Surprisingly, I think it'll all work out. Royce and his wife have agreed to make all the Markette performances. Dad will set up new gigs, handle the contracts and the business side of things. It's work he can do here while he recuperates. Later…" She shrugged. "Well, who knows? Boots and Spurs is looking for a new foreman. They've practically begged him to take the job."

Pink-and-yellow carnival lights dappled the face Mitch peered down to study. Amanda had changed in more ways than he'd given her credit for if she didn't mind her dad moving to town. "Are you okay with that?"

She gave a short laugh. "Now that he has someone else to boss, I'm kind of looking forward to having him around."

If she could forgive her dad after everything he'd done to screw up her life, maybe there was a chance for them after all. Mitch took a second to regroup before deciding Amanda's new and improved relationship with her father might work in their favor. At the head of the line, he handed over the roll of tickets he'd purchased back when he'd planned to pop the question at the top of the Ferris wheel.

The game had changed since then. His plans had

changed along with it. But tucking a twenty into the pocket of the attendant, he whispered, "You know what to do."

The boy had agreed to let them ride as long as they wanted. Until the carnival closed, if necessary. Mitch hoped it wouldn't take that long to convince Amanda they deserved another chance, but he wouldn't force her and he wouldn't beg. At the first sure sign that it was truly over between them, he'd cut the ride short and head for home, alone.

It might kill him, but he'd do it.

They took their seats, inches of space that might as well have been miles between them. The safety bar came down, pressing them into the hard plastic. Music played and the bucket jerked forward.

He resisted the urge to wrap one arm around the woman he'd loved for fifteen years. They rode higher, starting and stopping several times to let couples disembark and new ones take their places. For a while, the Ferris wheel turned in earnest. Knowing if he blew it this time, he'd never get another chance, Mitch sat quietly, his mind racing.

Words were how he made his living. Every day, he strung them together in order to convince this judge to issue a search warrant, that jury to convict. But sitting beside Amanda, he knew no brief he'd ever written, no summation he'd ever given a jury would mean as much as what he'd say to her in the next few minutes. He searched for eloquence and came up empty.

At last, he cleared his throat and said the only thing he knew that had a chance of making things right.

"I'm sorry." Two little words, but he'd never meant anything more in his life. Except, maybe, the three that followed them. "I love you."

He searched Amanda's face, hoping for some indication that she'd forgiven him. A sad smile formed on her lips. Her head slowly swung from side to side. "I love you, too, Mitch. But I'm afraid that's not enough."

"I'm not sure I understand," he said, just as their car swayed to a halt at the top of the Ferris wheel.

Amanda clamped one hand on her hat as wind whipped her hair across her face. Shifting in her seat, she turned toward him until the breeze caressed her curls the way Mitch's fingers itched to do.

"Before we ran into each other at the Saddle Up, I thought I had my life all figured out. I'd decided a family of my own wasn't in the cards. I didn't want to take the chance that I'd be the same kind of parent as my own mom and dad."

Mitch leaned forward. Words of reassurance formed on the tip of his tongue. Amanda would make a great mom. She'd never be the kind of parent either of hers had been. Before he could muster a syllable, she shushed him.

"Let me finish. That was before. Before I met you again." She smiled. "And Hailey." Amanda paused for a second. Though her expression didn't change, her voice turned solemn. "Thanks to both of you, I can see myself settling down one day. Having a family of my own." She wagged a finger back and forth between them. "But not us together."

Mitch pictured Amanda, her belly round with child. The crush of not sharing that dream with her was so great he had to ask, "If we love each other, why not?"

Her smile thinned. She stared into her lap. "You know why. I spent my childhood competing against my dad's career, vying to have some small part of his life. I swore I'd never put myself in that position again." Tears sparkled in the eyes she turned to his. "Your drive, your intensity make you the best of all possible prosecuting attorneys. I get that. But you have to admit it doesn't leave much time for your family. And with this new promotion, you'll have even less of it. That's not the life I want to live."

A sudden hope filled Mitch's heart. His fingers tightened on the safety bar. Slowly, he asked, "And what if I told you I turned down the job?"

Amanda's lips parted. "You…what?"

When he repeated himself, she squinted up at him. Wonder and something he didn't dare believe shone in her gaze.

"Why?" she asked. "Isn't it what you wanted? What you've been working for all this time?"

"I thought it was," he answered with a sigh. "I admit it—I've been a fool. I convinced myself I could have it all—a home, my daughter, a demanding job." He took a breath. "You taught me how badly I was failing. I saw in your eyes that Hailey deserved more than I was giving her. That my idea of family time one day a week wasn't enough. Becoming the next district attorney jeopardized even those few hours. So…" he shrugged "…I turned it down."

Sounds from the carnival faded into the background as he waited for some response from the woman he loved. Amanda didn't say a word. Didn't move a muscle. For the longest time she sat staring out over the midway. Finally, she turned to face him.

"I guess that changes things, doesn't it?" Her head tilted to one side, blond hair flowing like a river away from her face.

Mitch searched her features. His breath caught in his throat at the depth of emotion he saw swimming in her eyes. "It certainly does," he agreed. "I know I hurt you. But will you give me forever to make it up to you?"

"The rest of your life?"

At her whispered response, his mouth went so dry he could barely speak.

"Longer. Forever. Marriage, a house, a family—I want it all. With you. Only you."

She laughed then, a tinkling sound that washed away all his fears. "Why, Mitch Goodwin, if I'm not mistaken, that sounded an awful lot like a proposal."

"If it was, would you say yes?" He held his breath, waiting an eternity for her answer.

"If it was, I think I would."

The first of the carnival-closing fireworks burst over their heads, but Amanda's gaze never wavered. With colorful lights glinting in her eyes, she whispered the words he had waited a lifetime to hear.

"I love you, Mitch Goodwin." She pointed to the ground far below, where a white-haired couple watched the fireworks, their arms wrapped around each other. "I want that to be us."

"Me, too." He smiled, sliding closer. He had to hear her say it again. "So, you'll marry me? Soon?"

"I think fifteen years is long enough to wait, don't you?" Their eyes met, the love in hers enhanced by a sizzle of light from the sky as more fireworks exploded. "I don't want to wait another minute."

Neither did he. Unable to resist any longer, he swept his lips across hers. Tasting, plundering, holding, he promised her the world, his life, his everything.

They pulled apart at last, and Mitch signalled the ride operator. The Ferris wheel jerked into motion. Mitch wrapped his arms around the woman of his past, his present and his future, and pulled her close. He rained kisses onto Amanda's hair, then lifted her hand.

"You need a ring. Let's shop for one tomorrow." He grinned, wanting to buy her the biggest, shiniest one he could find. He imagined candlelight and wine. Saw himself going down on one knee for a proper proposal.

As usual, Amanda was one step ahead of him. She flexed her bare fingers. "A shopping trip might be nice, but only if Hailey can come, too. Your daughter does love her sparkles."

"Our daughter," Mitch corrected.

"Our daughter." Amanda snuggled into his embrace. "I like the sound of that."

Gently, he kissed the tip of her nose as the Ferris wheel slowed to a stop. Mitch stepped from the car and hurried to help Amanda out, not wanting to waste a minute of their time together. Having her next to him felt so right, and now he knew she'd be by his side for the rest of his life. He bent down and brushed a kiss across her lips.

His green-eyed beauty met his gaze. "Let's go home," she whispered.

Oblivious to the bright colors filling the night sky, Mitch wrapped his arm around Amanda's waist and steered them toward the start of their forever together.

* * * * *

HEART & HOME

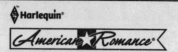

COMING NEXT MONTH
AVAILABLE JULY 10, 2012

#1409 AIDAN: LOYAL COWBOY
Harts of the Rodeo
Cathy McDavid

Can Aidan Hart put aside his responsibilities running the family ranch to deal with his surprise impending fatherhood? Find out in the first book of the Harts of the Rodeo miniseries!

#1410 A BABY ON THE RANCH
Forever, Texas
Marie Ferrarella

Abandoned by her husband, Kasey Stonestreet and her new baby move onto Eli Rodriguez's ranch, where the lifelong friends soon become lovers. *But what will happen when Kasey's husband returns?*

#1411 THE RENEGADE COWBOY RETURNS
Callahan Cowboys
Tina Leonard

Gage Phillips has spent his life as a renegade...until he finds out he has a daughter. Add a feisty Irish redhead who's a natural at motherhood and you have a recipe to tie down the formerly footloose cowboy!

#1412 THE TEXAS RANCHER'S VOW
Legends of Laramie County
Cathy Gillen Thacker

Matt Briscoe suspects the attractive artist hired by his father is hiding something from him. Jen Carson has sworn to keep the elder Briscoe's secret—but how can she, when she's falling in love with Matt?

Lively stories about homes, families and communities like the ones you know. This is romance the all-American way!

REQUEST YOUR FREE BOOKS!
2 FREE NOVELS PLUS 2 FREE GIFTS!

Harlequin®

American ★ Romance®

LOVE, HOME & HAPPINESS

YES! Please send me 2 FREE Harlequin® American Romance® novels and my 2 FREE gifts (gifts are worth about $10). After receiving them, if I don't wish to receive any more books, I can return the shipping statement marked "cancel." If I don't cancel, I will receive 4 brand-new novels every month and be billed just $4.49 per book in the U.S. or $5.24 per book in Canada. That's a saving of at least 14% off the cover price! It's quite a bargain! Shipping and handling is just 50¢ per book in the U.S. and 75¢ per book in Canada.* I understand that accepting the 2 free books and gifts places me under no obligation to buy anything. I can always return a shipment and cancel at any time. Even if I never buy another book, the two free books and gifts are mine to keep forever.

154/354 HDN FEP2

Name	(PLEASE PRINT)

Address	Apt. #

City	State/Prov.	Zip/Postal Code

Signature (if under 18, a parent or guardian must sign)

Mail to the **Reader Service:**
IN U.S.A.: P.O. Box 1867, Buffalo, NY 14240-1867
IN CANADA: P.O. Box 609, Fort Erie, Ontario L2A 5X3

Not valid for current subscribers to Harlequin American Romance books.

Want to try two free books from another line?
Call 1-800-873-8635 or visit www.ReaderService.com.

* Terms and prices subject to change without notice. Prices do not include applicable taxes. Sales tax applicable in N.Y. Canadian residents will be charged applicable taxes. Offer not valid in Quebec. This offer is limited to one order per household. All orders subject to credit approval. Credit or debit balances in a customer's account(s) may be offset by any other outstanding balance owed by or to the customer. Please allow 4 to 6 weeks for delivery. Offer available while quantities last.

Your Privacy—The Reader Service is committed to protecting your privacy. Our Privacy Policy is available online at www.ReaderService.com or upon request from the Reader Service.

We make a portion of our mailing list available to reputable third parties that offer products we believe may interest you. If you prefer that we not exchange your name with third parties, or if you wish to clarify or modify your communication preferences, please visit us at www.ReaderService.com/consumerschoice or write to us at Reader Service Preference Service, P.O. Box 9062, Buffalo, NY 14269. Include your complete name and address.

HAR11B

*Harlequin® American Romance® presents
a new installment in favorite author Tina Leonard's
miniseries* CALLAHAN COWBOYS.

Enjoy a sneak peek at
THE RENEGADE COWBOY RETURNS.

The secret to Gage Phillips's happy existence was ridiculously simple: stay far away from women, specifically those who had marriage on the mind.

He put his duffel on the porch of the New Mexico farmhouse and looked around. The rebuilding project he'd taken on for Jonas Callahan was perfectly suited to a man who loved solitude. Gage knew his formula for a drama-free, productive lifestyle was oversimplified to some, especially ladies who wanted to show him how much better his life could be with a good woman. But the fact that he was thirty-five and a die-hard, footloose cowboy only proved his formula was the best choice a man could ever make on this earth, besides choosing the right career and spending hard-earned cash on a dependable truck.

He hadn't always been die-hard and footloose. Fourteen years ago he'd been at the altar, and he'd learned a valuable lesson: marriage was not for him.

His friends were fond of saying he was just too much of a renegade to be tied down. Gage figured they might have a point. Fatherhood had been a late-breaking news bulletin for him about a year ago—what man was so busy traveling the country that he didn't know he had a daughter?

His ex, Leslie, convinced by her parents not to tell him about his child so they wouldn't have to share custody, had made a midlife conscience-cleansing decision to invite him to Laredo to tell him. He was pretty certain she had told him only because she was at her wit's end—and because Cat was apparently fond of making her mother's new boyfriend miserable.

The situation was messy.

"Excuse me," a woman said, and Gage jumped about a foot. "If you're selling something, I'm not buying, cowboy. And there's a No Trespassing sign posted on the drive, which I'm sure you noticed. And ignored."

He'd whipped around at her first words and found himself staring at a female of slender build, with untamable red hair, eyeing him like a protective mother hen prepared to flap him off the porch. Maybe she was the housekeeper, getting the place cleaned up for his arrival. Anyway, she seemed clear that he wasn't getting past the front door. He tried on a convincing smile to let her know he was harmless. "I'm not selling anything, ma'am. I'm moving in."

Who is this woman? Will she let Gage past the front door?

Find out in THE RENEGADE COWBOY RETURNS.
Available this July wherever books are sold.

This summer, celebrate everything Western
with Harlequin® Books!

www.Harlequin.com/Western